Hollow Beauty

ALSO BY KHRISTINA CHESS

STRAIGHT A's

Hollow Beauty

Khristina Chess

HOLLOW BEAUTY

This book is a work of fiction. All characters, events, and places are the product of the author's imagination, and any resemblance to real events, locales, or persons, living or dead, is entirely coincidental.

ISBN: 1500972509
ISBN-13: 978-1500972509

Contents

128 / 110 7

129 / 110 17

127 / 110 27

126 / 110 32

124 / 110 38

123.5 / 110 47

123 / 110 55

122 / 110 59

121 / 110 65

120 / 110 73

120 / 110 83

119.5 / 110 92

118 / 110 103

116 / 110 114

115 / 110 123

114 / 110 129

113.5 / 110 132

113 / 110 140

112 / 110 146

112 / 110 154

111.5 / 110 159

110 / 110 164

109/ 100 166

108/ 100 177

104 / 100 182

104.5 / 100 187

103 / 100 196

103 / 115 200

105 / 115 208

_____ 220

Discussion Questions.....................................226

Acknowledgements.......................................228

128 / 110

March 5

When I placed my order, I had no idea it would be my last medium curly fry and regular Coke for the next two months. If I'd known, I would have asked for a large.

I carried my tray to the condiments station for a glob of ketchup, extra salt, napkins, and a straw. Where to sit? My friend Tammy usually met me here on Thursdays for dinner after track practice, but she'd been out sick this week. I bit my lip for a moment before choosing an empty table by the window.

A bunch of guys from our school's baseball team sat in a booth along the wall. Brody Tipton, who I recognized from cross country, was sitting with them. Tall and wiry, he looked uncomfortably crowded in the molded plastic, especially with three other big guys. During the fall season, Brody and I had acted like goofballs together at practice, sometimes playing pranks and always goading one another as the top male and female runners on the team—but that only happened in cross country. Our paths rarely intersected inside the school. I hadn't talked to him since before Christmas, and now it was the first week of March.

Ravenous and with no one to talk to, I stared through the glass and devoured my fries. My favorites were the ones that formed tight, spiraling ringlets, and I searched through the pack to eat those first.

Cross country was the social misfit in the hierarchy of our high school's sports, but I enjoyed it much more than track and field. The longest event in track was only 3200m (two miles). I ran that and the 1600m (one mile), but I preferred the three miles of trails we ran in cross country, the cool fall air, the crunch of leaves under my tennis shoes, the rocky hills, and the muddy streams.

I started running 5K and 10K races with my big brother, Julian, when I was ten, and we hit every event in three counties. People probably became sick of calling our names and handing us trophies in our respective age groups. In middle school I joined the junior varsity cross country team. That had been Julian's senior year, so we only ran together for one year before he left for college, but the wooded trails around the high school still reminded me of him. Since entering graduate school, he didn't come home to visit very often.

Brody Tipton pulled out the chair across from me and plopped down, breaking my reverie. "Where's your sidekick?"

I swallowed before answering. "Tammy has bronchitis."

"I'm glad I ran into you here." His voice sounded serious. "There's something I wanted to ask you."

I nodded like we ran into each other all the time and this conversation was no big deal.

"Go to the prom with me," he said.

"Um," I said, confused and sure he was playing some kind of trick on me. I glanced over at the table of other boys to see if they were laughing. "That wasn't really a question."

"Just say yes, Olivia." He offered me that lopsided grin with dimples, and his blue eyes pleaded with me from beneath a long swag of honey blonde bangs.

"Yes…?"

"Awesome!" He looked ready to slap me with a high five.

I still couldn't believe what had just happened.

"Is this a joke or something?" The words flew out of my mouth before I thought better of them.

"No! Why would you think that?"

The puzzled expression on his face told me that I shouldn't have asked. "Nothing," I said, "it's just a weird surprise, that's all."

"If you don't want to go with me…"

"No, I do! Really, I just wasn't expecting you to ask." Fear went through me at the thought that he might withdraw his invitation. What kind of idiot was I? When Prince Charming asked you to the ball, you didn't stop and ask him, "Are you really sure you want to take *me*?"

Around us, the noise in the dining area was a roar. Nervously, I picked up another seasoned curly fry and swabbed it through the ketchup before popping it into my mouth.

"I know the prom's not until May," he said. "But you have to ask early to get a really *good* prom date." He winked at me, as if he thought I fell into that category. He flashed a smile of straight white teeth and cute dimples again. "And," he added, looking down at my tray, "that gives you a couple of months to lose a little weight."

My eyes popped open. "Lose weight?"

"For the dress." He laughed. "Oh come on, don't look at me like that! I know how all you girls like to slim down to fit into that perfect prom dress that's at least two sizes smaller than you usually wear and then spend at least a thousand dollars on pictures of yourselves in it."

"Not me. I'm a tomboy, remember?"

He nodded, not even listening. "For last year's prom, Erica lost something like twenty pounds. She looked amazing."

I felt suddenly conscious of the fact that my grungy hair was pulled up in a ponytail, and I was still wearing dirty sweats from practice.

"I know how competitive the two of you always were," he continued. "You're going to be beautiful. I know it."

The half-eaten burger and nearly empty package of fries cooled in front of me. I didn't want them anymore. Was *going* to be beautiful? Did he think I was *fat?*

The other guys on the baseball team dumped their trays and shuffled loudly over to our table. "Hey, Brody, we're heading out. You ready?"

"Yeah." He stood. "See you around," he said. He gave me another dazzling smile.

He loped away with that distinctive long runner's stride of his. Watching him go, I thought about the time last fall when he saved me from the team hazing at the creek.

10

Some of the boys had already thrown Tammy into the mud, and they had me in a full swing, arms and legs stretched long, while they shouted, "One, two, three…"

"No!" I squealed. "Don't do it!"

Brody appeared on the trail. I didn't know why he'd lagged behind the group, but suddenly he yelled, "Stop it! Put her down… on the bank!"

"Aw, come on, Brody!"

"We don't haze the girls," he said. "Not that way. Put her down."

Tammy stood there, dripping water and mud. "Where were you five minutes ago, Mr. Chivalrous?"

I felt myself being lowered to the ground. Girls weren't hazed, since when? And wasn't that sexist? Well, I wasn't going to argue this point at the moment—at least not while I was three feet from being thrown into a pit of mud and cold water.

I jumped up, and Tammy and I hurried up the trail, away from the boys, before they changed their minds. Plus, it looked like *someone* was going into the creek today, even if not one of us. They continued to argue among themselves.

"Are you okay?" I asked Tammy as we jogged. I worried because she was rubbing her arm.

Her tennis shoes sloshed with every step. "I hit my elbow on a stump or a rock or something, but other than that, yeah."

"Are you sure?"

"I'm ticked off more than anything."

I looked over my shoulder. Only their red shirts were visible through the leaves and underbrush now, but we could still hear raised voices.

"I think they're going to throw Brody into the creek," I said.

"They wouldn't dare."

And they didn't. Brody had everyone's respect. He was the top runner on the team this year, the senior, and the captain, and that meant that he sat where he wanted on the bus, took first place in line at our fast food pit stops, and got whatever else he wanted. Despite his royal status among us, he was nice. Sometimes when we walked a competitor's course before the race at an away meet, Brody strolled beside me and talked strategy—or just friend stuff. He flirted with all the girls, and he was so gorgeous that it was easy to fall in love with him.

Now, I had a prom date with him in two months. It was a dream come true. I looked down at my tray of remaining food and felt sick to my stomach.

At home later that night, I took a shower and got ready for bed. Wearing nothing but my underwear, I stood in front of the full-length bathroom mirror to take inventory. Wavy brown hair, plain brown eyes, average nose, flat lips, oblong face, and high cheekbones. With a critical eye, I also noticed that my thighs looked huge compared to the thin stilts that so many other girls in school called legs. And my hips and butt seemed too wide, like a big bubble back there. I'd always called my body "athletic." Words like "stocky" and "muscular" described my figure. I was the fastest girl on the track and cross country teams.

Muscular, stocky girls weren't *beautiful*, though. Skinny girls were. Girls like Erica Miller.

Last year in cross country, she and Brody had a thing, and they'd gone to the prom together in the spring before her graduation. In cross country, she hadn't been much of a competitor; she sprinted well but couldn't go the distance. In track, though, she beat me in the 1600m on multiple occasions because she could run a mile much faster than me. I hated losing to her.

Now that he'd reminded me, she *had* lost a lot of weight during track season, right before the prom.

Brody thought she'd looked amazing. But I could look amazing too. More amazing than her.

I stepped on the scale. After eating all that food and drinking that big soda, it said I weighed one hundred and twenty-eight pounds. I was five foot, four inches tall.

I combed my damp hair, turned off the bathroom light, and went to my bedroom. Losing weight fast was a problem because I didn't have an anorexic or bulimic bone in my body. Neither of those dieting solutions would work for me. I needed to lose weight before the prom and still be able to run in track meets. Running was my life. I didn't want to become a loser the way Erica had—just because of a stupid diet.

While my hair dried, I logged on my computer and did some quick searches for weight loss programs. Several familiar big names came up immediately; they ran commercials on TV every year around Christmas and New Year's with celebrity sponsors.

I spotted a name of one I'd never heard before: Blubber Busters.

According to the FAQ, Blubber Busters was an online-only group founded by a woman named Ana Marie. To fight the battle of the bulge, Ana Marie devised a simple Boot Camp program that advocated daily activity and online groups for support, charting progress, and renewing commitment.

It sounded like something I could do—and it was free. That whole "Boot Camp" thing scared me. What did they make you do? I clicked on the link and read the description. The first week of Boot Camp instructions didn't sound that unbearable:

1. Log your weight every day.
2. Log everything you eat.
3. Week one: eat only lite brands of chicken soup or chicken broth, hard-boiled eggs, watermelon, and bananas. Drink plenty of water or diet drinks.

Weight loss was guaranteed, at least two pounds the first week, unless I somehow managed to gorge myself on something like five dozen eggs every day for breakfast.

Next, I went to the Groups section. There were lots of forums to choose from. I chose the Teens list and lurked for awhile. Everyone's profile included their stats in the same format, like Bethany: 5'2", 143.5 / 101. This meant her height, current weight and goal weight.

Bethany: 5'2", 143.5 / 101: Down two more pounds this week. I'm always cold, but that means I'm burning calories, right? Ha, ha! I hope to reach my goal by summer bathing suit weather. I'm so tired of being fat.

Jane: 5'4", 113 / 100: You're doing great, Bethany. Keep up the good work, and you'll be beautiful for the beach.

Jane was as tall as I was, and her goal weight was one hundred pounds. I was thinking that my goal weight should be one hundred and ten, but should I adjust mine down to one hundred too? Would I still be too fat, even at one hundred and ten?

Dana: 5'7", 152.5 / 125: Is anyone else hungry? I'm starving all the time. I hate eggs, and chicken soup isn't cutting it for me. Help!

Molly: 5'0", 120 / 90: You need protein. Warm up a few extra grilled chicken chunks (low calorie) and add them to your soup. Don't go overboard. Carbs only make you hungry.

Dana: 5'7", 152.5 / 125: Thanks, I'll try that. I'm exercising twice a day, too. That's probably contributing to the hunger. I need to drink more water.

Exercising twice a day? I hadn't thought about that. I could run before school and then again at practice. I'd burn twice as many calories, improve my running, and easily reach my goal weight before the prom.

Two months. That's how much time I had to show Brody that I could lose more weight than Erica Miller and look stunning in the gown that I would need to save money to buy. I had some cash stashed away but wanted something really special. I wanted to transform myself from the tomboy in a ponytail into a total knockout.

It was the end of high school. My whole life was changing. Why not give myself a complete makeover in preparation for college? Just because I'd always been a tomboy and an athlete didn't mean I had to stay that way.

I pressed my hands against the slight curve of my belly and ran them along the outward slope of my hips and thighs. Maybe I wanted to become thinner for myself, not just because Brody had thrown down the gauntlet. Maybe I wanted to see if I could.

I read the Blubber Buster boards for an hour or so, but then I had to sign off. It was after midnight, and I had school tomorrow, then the Friday evening shift at work. I needed sleep.

129 / 110

March 6

On Friday morning as soon as I woke up, I stepped on the bathroom scale and discovered that I'd gained a pound overnight. How was that even physically possible? Did I go on a pre-dawn sleepwalking refrigerator raid?

Turning on my computer, I logged my weight and goal into my Blubber Busters profile.

Olivia: 5'4", 129 / 110: I'm starting Boot Camp today. Wish me luck!

I went to the bathroom, put on clothes, fixed my hair, and applied my makeup. When I came back to the computer again, a few people had already posted.

Molly: 5'0", 120 / 90: You don't need luck. The program works if you work the program. Really.

Lauren: 5'3.5", 117 / 105: I lost 5 pounds my first week of Boot Camp. You can do it! Just remember to eat only if you're hungry, and only eat the minimum that you need to feel satisfied. Don't overeat.

Jane: 5'4", 113 / 100: Drink lots of water!

In the kitchen, I searched the pantry for chicken noodle soup or broth since I didn't have time to boil any eggs. What we had was the chunky home-style brand, not lite, but it would have to do until I could ask Mom to pick up what I needed. At lunch, I could get bananas at the cafeteria and maybe some soup. I wasn't sure.

Morning classes passed in painful slow motion. I doodled flowers and vines in my notebook. Very few classmates paid rapt attention to the teacher. We were seniors on the home stretch toward college, waiting to get our acceptance letters in the mail and trying to keep our grades up for the last few months when all any of us really wanted to do was play.

In Spanish class, I sat beside my best friend, Alice. She rattled with costume jewelry—necklaces, earring, bangles, watches—all at the same time. She made a lot of it herself. Until Brody's comment about losing weight, I'd never really given her size (or mine) much thought, but now I noticed that Alice was neither athletic nor skinny, but a soft chubby. She'd never said or done anything to make me think that she worried one minute about her weight or what anyone thought about her body, but I was confident that if she knew what Brody had said, she'd be furious.

Alice looked awesome the way she was, but after staring at my thighs last night, I agreed with Brody's assessment of me: a little fluffy. Too many curves and not enough angles. I needed to shed some weight before the prom, and I liked having a specific goal to focus on. Nineteen pounds. It was like being in training.

On the track, it was about shaving off seconds and trying to reach a personal best time. Winning against the opposing team—and my own—was critical, but it was always the clock that stayed ahead of me in every race and motivated me toward a new goal.

I had a feeling that the scale might work the same way: pound by pound, day by day, inch by inch.

Challenges didn't scare me.

As students continued shuffling into the room before the bell, I leaned over and whispered to Alice, "Brody asked me to senior prom last night."

"Brody *Tipton?*" Her mascara-laden eyes widened.

"The one and only." I grinned. "Maybe we can get a limo together—me and Brody, and you and Nash."

"Maybe." She shrugged and tossed her hair over her shoulder. "Although he might be planning to share a limo with *his* friends, not yours. You might be going to the prom with the baseball team."

I made a face. "We'll see about that."

Mrs. Oren took that moment to walk into the room in her three-inch heels and begin class. She was a tiny Puerto Rican woman with long black hair, and she spoke in rapid, staccato sentences. I'd been taking Spanish for three years and still struggled to understand her sometimes.

After class, I walked with Alice to the cafeteria, where we met Nash. He and Alice had been together since freshman year, but he still treated her like they'd just met. He took a lunch tray off the stack and handed it to her. He put his hand on her lower back and let her step in front of him in line. He set her favorite desserts on her tray and nibbled on her ear when teachers weren't looking. He called her endearments like "sweetheart" and "lovey."

More than anything, I wanted the kind of relationship that Alice and Nash had. I wanted to know how it felt to fall madly in love and to spend my hours consumed by thoughts of another person—and have that reciprocated. To be able to spend hours in his company, delighted by his every word, constantly laughing, and to know that our time apart would be agony until we could be together again. To read one another's minds and finish each other's sentences. To be wrapped in his arms and kissed so passionately that I knew beyond any shadow of a doubt that he was the one for me. To see him gazing at me with the same raw emotion.

As if to illustrate my point, Nash fed Alice one of the tater tots on his tray. She smiled, stood on tiptoe, and kissed him.

It was nauseating.

That's what I wanted—true love.

When I arrived at the Grace Lake Diner for my Friday night shift, it was already busy. I grabbed a tub and headed into the dining room to bus tables that the waitresses hadn't had time to clean yet. The dishwashing machine waited for me in the kitchen. Usually Sally, the cook, kept up with dishes until I showed up for the evening shift, but on Fridays, a backlog of dirty tubs waited for me.

"I'm running low on platters," Sally said when I returned to the kitchen. She was a woman in her mid-forties—about the same age as my mom—and she made her job look like a dance. In her cook's white uniform and hairnet, she twirled between the steam tray, grill, fryers, and broiler in a well-timed waltz that had the rest of us scurrying to keep up with her.

"I'll put them through." I sorted through the tubs and loaded the tray with as many plates and platters as I could find, scraping food and paper into the garbage can while I worked. Dishes came out so hot that my fingers burned to touch them.

I made minimum wage, but cash was cash. Mom had found me a used car and paid half the insurance on the condition that I pay the other half and buy my own gas. I took as many weekend shifts as Mr. Lee would give me and already had a savings account built up. Since my best friend was "In Love," it wasn't like I had a huge social nightlife.

How much money would a prom dress cost? Plus shoes and accessories—there were all kinds of cute things to spend money on.

Suddenly, the cooler door opened, which was weird because Sally was jitterbugging at the grill, and I knew both of the waitresses were in the dining room. A boy walked out. Or rather, limped. He looked around my age. Our eyes met as he carried a jug of coleslaw to the counter.

Sally looked over her shoulder. "Oh hey, Olivia, meet the new prep cook, Ross. Ross, this is Olivia, our dishwasher."

"Hi." He offered a smile.

"Hi. You picked an awful first night to start," I said. "Friday nights are the worst."

"I enjoy challenges."

I returned the smile. "Then you've definitely come to the right place."

"Enough with the chitchat," Sally said. "I need that slaw. Order's up."

Ross unscrewed the lid and looked around the counter for the scoop. I left my station to show him where it was.

"Thanks," he said.

His eyes were hazel, flecked with green and brown and even some violet, and his dark brown hair looked naturally curly, wild and unruly, falling almost to his collar. A scar, barely visible, traced his hairline from his right temple to his ear. It looked like a question mark.

"Her bark's worse than her bite," I mumbled.

"Don't bet on it," Sally called out. "Move it, Ross. And Olivia, I want my gravy pot."

I rolled my eyes and scrambled to the sink. All the cook's pots and pans were hand-washed in the big basin because they didn't fit in the dishwashing machine.

The entire shift went that way: run to the dining room to clear tables, keep the dishwashing machine loaded, stack clean dishes and glasses in their places, sort silverware, and wash pots. Whenever I had the chance, I snuck peeks at Ross. Where was he from? Was he in school, or had he graduated? In a Friday night shift, there wasn't time for a lot of conversation, and Sally barked at anyone who tried because it broke her concentration.

So instead I watched how his biceps flexed and his shoulders moved beneath his tee-shirt as he carried gallon jugs of ranch dressing, coleslaw, and other ingredients around the kitchen for Sally, and after awhile I started wishing that she'd ask him to carry something really heavy.

At the end of the evening, Ross and I helped Sally clean the steam table and grill. We mopped floors in the bakery and kitchen. We burned boxes and lugged garbage to the dumpster at the far end of the building.

When it was finally time to go home, I walked out to the parking lot with Ross. It was dark except for one streetlight. The only cars left in the parking lot were ours, Sally's, and Mr. Lee's. We stopped a few feet beyond the front door. "So how'd you like your first day?" I asked.

He shrugged. "It's a job. You have something black on your chin."

"Probably grease." I swiped my face with my sleeve. "Work hazard."

We looked at one another, and since he was quite a bit taller, his chin tilted down toward my face at this close proximity. After watching him for an entire shift and thinking of all sorts of questions to ask, I was struck mute once we were alone together.

"Thanks for all your help tonight," he said. "It's going to take me awhile to remember where everything is."

"No problem. I was new once, too."

"When do you work again?"

"Tomorrow afternoon," I said.

"Me too. I guess we'll see each other then."

I nodded. His voice was nice—deep and quiet. My instant attraction to him was disarming because he was so *not* my type. I liked the lean and lanky athletic, fair-haired boys like Brody Tipton. Except for his height, Ross was the complete opposite. Yet for one insane moment, I wanted to reach up and touch those wild brown curls at the nape of his neck.

Instead, I tried to step around him and head in the direction of my car. He stopped me with another question. "Where do you go to school?"

"Fairview. You?"

"Lakeside."

I made a *tsk* sound. "Oh no, you're one of *those*."

"You have a problem with Lakeside?" His mouth quirked up, and his hazel eyes seemed to dance with amusement.

"The girls on your track team can be... petty."

"In what way?" He raised his eyebrows.

"Let's just say there are certain courtesies you'd expect from everyone, even if the track meet isn't going your way." Some things about girls' bathrooms and stalls without toilet paper were not topics of conversation to exchange with good-looking boys you'd just met. I gave my car a longing look.

"So, you're in track," he said. "A runner or field sports?"

"Runner, 1600m and 3200m."

"A *distance* runner. Impressive." He nodded and hooked his thumbs in the pockets of his jeans.

Those wild curls of his kept distracting me. What was *wrong* with me? Maybe it was a thing about missing my seasoned curly fries or something. Yeah, that was it; I was just hungry. His ringlets reminded me of my favorite food.

"I run cross country too," I volunteered.

"You're a girl who likes the mud?" This news seemed to delight him.

"Um, I like to run on trails in the woods, and sometimes I get muddy, but other than that..."

"I like to ride dirt bikes. And also go caving."

I thought about tight, dark places… and bats. I shook my head. "Doesn't sound appealing."

"Don't knock it until you try it. There are hidden treasures beneath the earth. Worlds undiscovered."

"What if you get lost?"

"You have equipment to help you avoid that, and you always go with a group. Are you off on Sunday afternoon?"

"Yeah…" If he was going to invite me on a caving adventure, he should stop right now.

"My grandfather owns some land—quite a bit actually—and I like to go dirt bike riding out there on weekends. You interested in taking a ride with me?"

"On your dirt bike?"

"Yes." He gave me a crooked, goofy grin that somehow looked very hot to me.

"In the woods?"

"Yes." Still grinning.

I folded my arms across my chest. "I don't even know your last name, and you want me to ride into the woods with you, alone, on a dirt bike?"

"So if I told you my last name was Lector, you wouldn't go?"

"Is it?"

"No." He laughed. "It's Bellows. I promise I'm not a serial killer or psychopath. I'm just asking a pretty girl to go for a ride on my dirt bike."

I blushed at being called pretty.

"What do you say?" he asked.

I sighed and shook my head. "I'd like to, but unfortunately, I can't this Sunday because I already have plans with my mom and grandparents. Maybe next Sunday, if you want?"

"Next Sunday, then. Goodnight, Olivia." He turned and kind of lurched toward his car. I wondered what was wrong with his leg but was afraid to ask. I pulled my keys out of my purse and headed toward my own car.

I unlocked my door, started the engine, and drove home. I couldn't believe I'd just agreed to hang out with this new guy that I hardly knew. Well, we were just going for a ride on a dirt bike. A friend thing. It wasn't a date or anything.

127 / 110

March 9

It was still dark on Monday morning when I went outside to run hill sprints. Frost crunched beneath my sneakers as I walked across the lawn to the end of the driveway, where I stretched beside the mailbox for a few minutes. Even in northern Alabama in March, it was freezing, only in the upper-twenties, and the pre-dawn sky was full of stars. For a moment, I missed Julian so much it hurt; my brother and I used to love running together in the morning like this, when the whole neighborhood was quiet and still.

The steep hill in front of my house was about an eighth of a mile long. I walked down the road until the pavement flattened out, turned, and took several deep breaths to psych myself up. Hill sprints were the worst.

I sprinted to the top.

Gasping, my breath on fire inside my lungs, I turned, walked down the road again, and repeated until I'd completed eight of them. Climbing higher, pushing farther—I felt strong, fast, and powerful. Most track girls didn't bother with hill training because the track was flat, but our cross country coach made us do these at least once a week. Hill sprints made me a better runner in any kind of condition.

After the last one, I jogged another mile for cool-down before returning to the house for a shower. I felt good enough to go three miles, but we'd probably run at least that much in this afternoon's practice. No sense in overdoing it.

I went in the house and began stripping my layers of sweats, hat, and gloves. My stomach growled for breakfast: two hard-boiled eggs and a banana to start. The good thing about this diet was that I was allowed to eat enough that I didn't go hungry, but the bad thing was boredom. I already missed my curly fries and regular Coke.

Beauty had a price.

Mom emerged from the living room with a cup of coffee. "You were outside?"

"Yeah, I decided to go for a run."

She frowned. "Don't you have practice tonight?"

"I did some hill work. Our meets start this week. I want to be ready."

"Isn't it cold out there?"

"Freezing," I agreed, kicking off my shoes and walking over to the refrigerator. "But it's exhilarating, too."

"If you say so. Do you want me to fix you something for breakfast?"

Usually, she cooked French toast, pancakes, bacon, or anything else I wanted.

"No, I'm just going to have a couple of eggs this morning." I took two of the hard-boiled eggs out of the bowl.

"What's with this new diet of yours?"

"I'm in training. Building lean muscle, slimming down."

"You don't need to slim down," Mom said.

I ducked my head. Mom didn't diet. Her waist had vanished years ago. Her breasts rested on her stomach, and her stomach was considerable.

"I wanted to try something high protein and healthy," I said. "Maybe it will give me an edge on the track."

"You don't need some weird diet to give you an edge."

"Since when did eggs become weird, Mom?" I sat at the table with my breakfast and cracked the first shell.

She watched me for a few minutes and then returned to the living room with her coffee. As soon as I finished breakfast, I headed to the shower, hurrying because my early morning run had put me behind schedule. I made it to school before the first bell.

After first period, I went to my locker to retrieve a forgotten notebook.

"Hey, Olivia."

I jumped and almost dropped my books. Brody circled around me and leaned against the lockers. His blonde bangs hung over his sleepy eyes at an angle. He gave me a dimpled grin.

"Oh! Hi." I managed a smile, grabbed the notebook, and slammed the door before he could look inside.

"What are you hiding in there?" he asked.

A huge and embarrassing mess. "My Edward and Jacob action-figure collection."

"What?"

I shook my head. "Joking, never mind."

He shrugged, and his blue eyes locked with mine. "Your first meet's tomorrow, isn't it?"

"Yeah, against Victory. They're not too bad." It took effort to form coherent sentences around him—at least in this setting. I wished we were walking and talking in the woods, where conversation between us had been easier.

"You'll do great, I'm sure." He kept looking down at me and smiling.

I blushed. "I don't know. Every race is different."

"Well, I just saw you over here and wanted to wish you good luck."

"Oh, um, thanks."

"See you around." He pushed away from the lockers and straightened to his full height.

"Yeah."

He turned and took long strides down the hall. I watched a few seconds before turning and heading in the opposite direction, toward the science wing. I couldn't believe Brody Tipton had just stopped and talked to me. That had *never* happened before. Our paths didn't even cross in the same hall, so he must have sought me out, not simply "noticed" me over here. Was this because he'd asked me to the prom? Was he going to start talking to me more often now, or was that wishful thinking?

I went to my Physics class and took a seat. I liked this class, but today I had trouble paying attention because I kept daydreaming about Brody and me falling in love. I pictured his perfect face bending towards mine, eyes half closed, lips pressing softly against mine, kissing me so passionately that there was no doubt that he was the one for me. I imagined the warmth of his strong arms around me as we danced together at the prom. I fantasized that we began dating and spent hours together, just having fun. In one fantasy, he surprised me with a single, long-stemmed red rose after first period. Or better yet, he played the piano and sang love songs to me. I thought about my favorite parts of romantic movies and put the two of us into those scenes.

Physics class never went by so fast.

126 / 110

March 10

Our track meet against Victory was at home under hostile weather conditions. Frigid northern winds blew steadily, and overcast skies threatened rain all afternoon. Too soon, the dreaded moment came when I had to take off my warm sweats and compete in the 1600m.

At the starter gun, we sprinted as a pack for the first curve, with the top runner on Victory's team immediately taking the lead. Since the wind was so bad, I willingly fell in behind her and rested in the pocket. She never slowed down. The entire 1600m felt like a one-mile sprint. When I kicked in for the final push around that last 400m lap, the lead runner on the Victory team stayed with me until we rounded the last corner, and I passed her, winning by only three seconds. I didn't like cutting it that close.

I worried that she'd challenge me in the 3200m too. Maybe that event was her strongest.

"You have nothing to worry about," my friend Tammy said. She was a tall, round-faced girl with straight bangs across her forehead. "You took everything she had during that last lap."

I shivered in my sweats. "That wind felt like a giant hand, pushing me backwards."

"It's no picnic on the pole vault either."

"I heard you earned a personal best. Congratulations," I said. "I knew you could do it!"

"Thanks." Tammy stamped her feet and rubbed her arms.

"I thought you were never going to get over that bronchitis. I'm glad you're finally feeling better."

"Me too. I hate being sick."

I hadn't thought about Erica Miller at all since track last year, but ever since Brody had asked me to the prom and challenged me to lose some weight, her name had been floating around in my mind. The pace of that 1600m reminded me of how races used to go with Erica. She was lightning fast.

"Do you remember Erica Miller?" I asked.

"Sure. Who doesn't? Why?"

"I was thinking how fast that other girl is, like Erica."

Tammy nodded. "Yeah, I can see that."

I nibbled the tip of my tongue for a moment. "Didn't Erica and Brody Tipton date for awhile?"

"Oh yeah, most of her senior year. Don't you remember?"

"I thought so." I nodded. Then I blurted out. "He asked me to the prom last week, and I said yes."

"Oh, really? Congratulations!"

"I couldn't believe it at first. I thought it was a joke or something."

We stood there for a few minutes and watched them set up for the hurdles.

After a moment, Tammy gave me a sideways look and lowered her voice. "I think Brody cheated on Erica a couple of times. That's the rumor, anyway."

"Really?" I didn't know anything about this. "With who?"

"Hannah, for one." Tammy held up her index finger and raised her eyebrows. "I couldn't believe Erica took him back after that. And then on top of it, Erica lost all that weight in the spring, right before the prom. Do you remember? She got so skinny."

"I started beating her in the 1600m," I said. "*That's* what I remember."

"And right after the prom, he dumped her for that other girl... what was her name?" Tammy snapped her fingers. "Luna, or something like that. I heard he was cheating then, too."

I looked at the blacktop. Tammy obviously didn't have a high opinion of Brody.

"He definitely flirted with all the girls on the cross country team," I agreed.

"Especially you." Tammy bumped my shoulder. "I don't think he would have stopped them from throwing *me* into the creek that day."

"Yes, he would have," I insisted. "He's a nice guy."

She made a face. "I'm not so sure about that."

"You must think that my going with him is a terrible mistake."

"It's a dance," Tammy said. "Dress up, take pictures, drink punch, and have a few laughs. Just don't fall for him."

She was probably right, but part of me wanted it to be more than just a dance. A big part. In fact, I thought I might have already fallen for him, and so far all he'd done was lean against my locker and smile at me.

Coach Wilby walked over and stood between us. He was a stout man. Tammy looked down on him, and I saw him eye-to-eye. "You girls ready to run?" he asked.

"Yes, sir," we said in unison.

He wore a knit hat to keep his balding head warm. His brown eyes bulged, sort of like a frog's. "All stretched out, then?" he asked.

I grabbed an ankle and stretched my quadriceps. "Still pretty loose from my last race."

"Any more problems with those shin splints?" he asked Tammy.

"Nope, all better." She hopped on tiptoes a few times for demonstration.

"Great, because we need first and second place," he said. "Can I count on both of you?"

"Yes, sir," we said.

The girl who challenged me in the 1600m took her place in the 3200m race. I planned to use the same strategy, following behind her to let her break the wind, but she didn't keep pace. I passed her after two laps and kept going. My legs felt strong. I felt like a prized racehorse, rounding the corner in the Kentucky Derby, feeling the blood pounding in my veins and the roar of the crowd in my ears. One of my favorite movies was about a race horse that ended up becoming a Triple Crown champion because a few people believed in him. He was smaller than the others and had no business winning against those giant thoroughbreds, but he did anyway.

Sometimes I felt like an underdog, too. My dad had left when I was a baby, so it was just my mom, Julian, and me. It seemed like we were always at a disadvantage in some way, but then I found running. I could win. On a track, in a race, for a few miles of running, I could be special. It didn't matter that I didn't have a pedigree or a dad.

By the final lap of the 3200m, I was far enough ahead of the pack that I didn't need to push, but I sprinted the final lap anyway. The stopwatch was a constant competitor I could never beat; it was always one second ahead of my personal best time.

Tammy and I brought first and second place to Coach Wilby, and our team won the meet.

That night before bed, I logged into Blubber Busters to read postings from the group.

Olivia: 5'4", 126 / 110: I'm down 3 pounds so far this week. Boot Camp is working for me. I won my two events in our track meet tonight, and it felt great to be so strong, full of energy, and yet light on my feet. I felt like I could have gone another mile.

Lauren: 5'3.5", 116 / 105: Double congratulations on the win and the race. Keep up the good work. Success leads to more success.

Ana Marie: 5'10" 117/120: Great job! Three pounds is awesome!

Molly: 5'0", 121 / 90: You're inspiring me, Olivia. I wish I could run. Anyone have tips for breaking through a plateau? I can't seem to get past 120.

Jane: 5'4", 111 / 100: I'd love to hear the answer to that one, too. Sometimes my goal just seems impossible.

The posts went on and on, voices reaching out into the void for contact with other human beings who might understand and share in the same struggles with weight. I read for a half hour or so. All I could think about was food. That's all any of us thought about.

One can of light chicken noodle soup for dinner had not been enough, especially with all the running. My stomach growled. I liked the lightness of being hungry, though. I already felt thinner.

I turned out the light and closed my eyes and tried to imagine myself in a prom dress—something vibrant and silky and clingy. Something that would make me look beautiful.

124 / 110

March 13

By Friday morning, after a full week of Boot Camp, I'd lost five pounds. Thrilled by my progress, I dressed in sweats, and just as I'd done every morning that week, I went outside before school and ran hill sprints, followed by a mile cool-down jog. Then I ate a hard-boiled egg for breakfast. Following the same routine made the diet easier. No thinking, no deviations, just do it.

After first period, Brody stopped by my locker again and gazed down at me. "Hey Olivia."

This time, I didn't startle as easily at the sound of his voice. Also, my locker was no longer full of used tissues, crumpled papers, candy wrappers, and other junk. Everything looked neat and tidy. I left the door open. See? No weird action figures or posters of teen heartthrobs hanging in there.

"Hi," I said.

"Congratulations on the win yesterday. I heard you ran really well." He flashed those disarming dimples at me.

"Thanks." I felt my cheeks heating under his stare. "You wouldn't believe how cold it was. It was brutal yesterday."

"Spring will be here before you know it." His blue eyes appraised me intently, and he lowered his voice. "And the prom."

"I know."

"I'm looking forward to it."

"Me too."

He cocked his head to the side and furrowed his brow. "You look different."

I shrugged. "I took your advice."

"What advice was that?"

"You know, for the pictures. I've lost five pounds so far."

Recognition appeared on his face. "That's what it is! You look really, really great! Keep it up." He looked like he wanted to say something else but then realized the time. "See you around?"

"Sure."

We hurried in opposite directions for class, and I barely made it to physics class before the bell. What was that? Wonderful, that's what. The prom was too far away. I wanted to dance with him right now. I wanted him to lower his head while we stood at the lockers and kiss me right there.

Spanish class was my only chance during the day to talk with Alice alone, without Nash. At lunch, they always came as a package deal, and even though it had been this way for years, and even though I liked Nash a lot, sometimes I really just needed her to myself.

"Have you heard anything negative about Brody?" I asked Alice before Mrs. Oren came into the room.

"Negative how?" She wore dangling moonstone earrings today with a matching necklace. The handmade stonework in the necklace was exquisite.

"That he's a cheater or anything like that."

"No, why?"

"Tammy was telling me some stuff about how he was last year when he was dating Erica, and I just wondered if you knew anything."

Alice shrugged. "I always thought he was a nice guy."

"I know, me too. I don't know why she thinks that."

"Maybe she's jealous," Alice suggested.

"You think?"

"You said he flirted with all the girls in cross country. Maybe she has a crush on him too."

I hadn't thought of that. "But we're friends."

"Friends get jealous of friends. That can be the worst."

Mrs. Oren came into the classroom with an armful of folders. She looked at us over the rims of her glasses and began speaking in rapid-fire Spanish. "Be quiet," she said (loose translation).

Throughout the class, I thought about what Alice had said. I didn't like to think that Tammy would mislead me about a guy because of jealousy, but I also wanted her to be wrong about him. When he leaned against the lockers and gazed down at me with those intense blue eyes, with his honey blond hair falling across his forehead that way, I wanted to believe that we might fall in love with each other.

Watching him lope away from me down the hall, well, I thought I was already pretty smitten with him.

At lunch with Alice and Nash, I told them about my encounter with Brody, and they agreed. "You have it bad," Alice said.

"What do you think his sudden visits to my locker mean? Do you think he might like me too?"

"He definitely likes you," Nash said. His real name was Graham, but he gave himself the nickname, Nash, for his favorite city, Nashville. He was a beanpole with several tattoos on his arms, back, and legs—mostly action heroes, fantasy characters, swords, and related imagery. He wore his hair shaved to about an inch. He'd already received an acceptance letter into MIT.

"Do you know whether or not he's a player?" I asked Nash.

"No. But he doesn't seem the type."

"What's the type?" Alice wanted to know.

Nash looked around the cafeteria and after a moment pointed at one of the geekiest boys in our class. "Player."

"Get out of here," I said.

"You don't know what you're talking about," Alice said.

"I'm telling you." Nash nodded. He continued looking around the room and found another boy of similarly questionable social abilities. "Player."

"Maybe you don't know what that term means," I suggested.

He threw his hands in the air. "Don't take my word for it, then. Think what you want."

I peeled my banana, smiling.

Alice frowned at me. "Is that really all you're eating? A banana?"

"Yeah."

"Are you on some kind of diet or something?"

I decided to tread lightly with her on this because she would disapprove of Blubber Busters and my reason for doing it.

"I'm trying to eat healthier for track," I said.

"You look like you've lost weight."

"Maybe a couple of pounds. I've toned up."

Alice made a face. "You're skinny enough."

I shrugged, feeling annoyed, and took a bite of my banana. My weight wasn't anyone's business. Why did people think it was okay to tell others that they were "too skinny" to their face? It sure as heck was taboo to go around telling people they were "too fat."

"I think you look great," Nash said.

"Thank you," I said. "I appreciate that."

"How'd you do last night, anyway?" he asked.

"I won both 1600 and 3200. And we won the meet overall. Tammy earned a personal best on the pole vault."

Conversation shifted to the cold weather during the event and away from my diet. Alice continued sending me sour looks as I slowly finished my banana, but I didn't care. Members on the message boards talked about saboteurs in our lives who tried to keep us from dieting because they were jealous. I never thought Alice would be one of them, but like she said earlier, when it came to jealousy, friends could be the worst.

I guess I needed to get advice about how to hide my diet better because I still had fourteen pounds to lose before reaching my goal weight.

When I arrived at the diner Friday night, Ross had already started his shift. Controlled chaos ruled the kitchen. The special was all-you-can-eat catfish. Sally managed the grill and all three fryers. She'd assigned Ross to keeping a steady supply of fish battered and the dishes of coleslaw filled for orders.

"Where have you been?" Sally roared at me.

"I'm ten minutes early!" I protested. "And I was at school."

"I only have five clean platters left and ten orders to fill."

I rolled up my sleeves and set to work on the tubs of dirty dishes. Every now and then, I snuck a glance in Ross's direction. Sally had him covered in flour and egg batter. I grinned.

"Something funny?" he asked, catching me.

"You look... a mess." *Yummy* had been the word that actually came to mind.

"Thank you for that keen observation."

"I like a cook who gets into his work," Sally said. "Too bad we don't see more of that in you, Olivia. You're much too clean over there."

"My work uses hot water and soap," I said. "What do you expect?"

The fast pace made the evening pass quickly. By closing time, I was exhausted. I helped Ross and Sally clean the kitchen, take out the garbage, and mop the floors. The three of us left the building together.

"Good work, you two," Sally said. High praise, coming from her. "See you tomorrow. Don't be late."

"I'm off tomorrow, remember?" Ross said.

"Oh yeah. Well, you're here, right, Olivia?"

"Always."

Ross and I lingered in the parking lot while she unlocked her car, waved, and drove away.

"I think I'm starting to get the hang of this place," he said, shifting his weight to his good leg.

"It does grow on you."

"Are we still on for Sunday afternoon?"

I ran my hands through my hair, pulling it away from my face and off my sweaty neck. I couldn't wait to get home and take a hot shower. "Sure. Do I meet you here, or what?"

His eyes followed my hands up to my hair and then slid down my neck, slowly, before returning to my eyes. The movement of his gaze felt deliberate, as if he wanted me to know I'd distracted him with my hair, and it pleased him.

I dropped my hands, unnerved.

"I'll have the truck, and the dirt bike will be on a trailer," he said. "We'll meet here, then drive to my grandfather's farm and ride there." His hazel eyes sparkled with excitement. Clearly, he couldn't wait to get me on that motorcycle.

My thoughts kept stumbling over that look he'd given me as his eyes trailed down my neck. I felt something low and fluttery in my belly.

"Do you have an extra helmet?" I asked. To my own ears, my voice seemed a little strangled and not my own.

"Yes."

I chewed on my lower lip and didn't say anything.

He watched my mouth for a moment before saying, "You seem nervous about something."

He made me nervous.

"I've never ridden on a motorcycle before," I said. "They seem dangerous."

His deep voice took on a soothing tone. "I won't do anything reckless, Olivia. You're safe with me."

"Uh-huh." Nothing about him seemed very safe to me.

"What, you don't trust me?" He raised his eyebrows with amusement.

"I don't *know* you," I pointed out. "You goad Sally in the kitchen, which is definitely reckless behavior."

"You told me her bark is worse than her bite."

That made me laugh and lightened the tension between us. "That doesn't mean you should poke the bear."

"That bear is a pussycat in disguise."

"If you mess something up in her kitchen, she will eat you for lunch."

"Noted." He smirked. Definitely not a guy with a strong sense of self-preservation. "So… do you work every weekend?" he asked.

"Yeah, I try to get as many hours as I can. During the week, I can't really take a shift because of school, but Mr. Lee usually schedules me for Friday and Saturday nights and Sunday breakfast."

"When do you have fun?"

"Fun? What's that?" I shook my head. "I like to read, which I do all the time, and run."

"Running is fun?"

"Haven't you ever heard of the runner's high?"

"Is that a real thing?"

"Yeah. A cool morning with my iPod and my thoughts, feeling strong and good, is a great high."

"What do you think about?" He looked like he really wanted to know.

I paused and gave it some thought. "My mind just wanders over all kinds of things, I guess. Life questions. Little things. Books I'm reading. Whatever. When I'm running, my mind is free. It's the most peaceful feeling. It's hard to describe." I yawned. Covering my mouth, I mumbled, "Sorry."

"No, it's late." He straightened. "We should go. You have to work tomorrow, and I'm going caving with a group of friends."

"Sounds fun, I guess."

"It will be," he said.

"Okay, so I'll see you here on Sunday afternoon."

I unlocked my car and drove home. My eyes felt heavy, and I kept yawning. I felt uneasy, though, about whether this dirt bike thing had been such a good idea. With that long, lingering look, it seemed that Ross might have ideas beyond *just a friend thing*. I needed to set him straight, and soon.

123.5 / 110

March 15

The Sunday morning breakfast shift at the diner was steady but not terrible. I liked working this shift because at the end, I didn't have to clean up the kitchen; that job fell to the evening dishwasher's shift. I got off at two, changed clothes, and met Ross at the counter. He sat there with a glass of Coke, wearing jeans and a long-sleeved checkered shirt, rolled up to the elbows. He looked every bit the broad, muscular farm boy.

"You ready to go?" he asked.

"Is this okay?" I pointed at my jeans and sweatshirt.

"Are you okay with getting those dirty?"

"Yep."

"Then you're perfect." He left a tip by the glass and slid off the stool. I followed him out to the parking lot. A white four-wheel-drive Chevy truck in serious need of a washing waited for us. The dirt bike rode on a low trailer behind the truck.

Ross escorted me to the passenger side and opened the door. The seats seemed at least six feet above the ground. He pointed to a handle above the door. "Step on the running board and use that to pull yourself up."

I grabbed the handle and swung into the seat. Ross closed the door behind me and made his way around the truck. He climbed into the driver's seat without difficulty and turned the key. The diesel engine roared to life.

He reached forward and turned on the radio. "What kind of music do you like?" he asked.

"Country," I said, fastening my seat belt.

"You?" He pushed one of the pre-set stations, and a familiar artist began singing at low volume.

"You too, apparently."

He pulled onto the main road. "I like all kinds of music," he said. "Country, pop, classical…"

"Classical, really?" This surprised me.

"Really."

"Huh. I learn something new about you every day."

"Same here." His deep voice seemed extra low. "I never would have pinned you for a country girl."

I cleared my throat. "So, how long's it going to take us to get there?"

"You in a hurry?"

"No, just wondering." How long were we going to be here in close quarters, talking like this?

"About twenty minutes."

"Oh." I fiddled with the seat belt harness and stared out the window. That was a long time for me to make a fool of myself.

"You mentioned that you like to read a lot," he said. "What are you reading right now?"

"A book by Laurie Halse Anderson."

"I like some of her stuff. You ever read John Green?"

"I love him," I said. "I've read everything he's written."

"I've read a couple. I like science fiction/fantasy best."

"I liked *Hunger Games* and *Harry Potter*, but I'm not a huge science fiction fan."

"Then you just haven't read the right book yet."

We traded many other authors and titles. Ross gave the synopsis of his favorite science fiction story ever. Then I told him about my favorite book. My voice kept rising with excitement because Ross was the first person to really share my passion for reading. Not even Alice and Tammy could talk books with me.

Time passed quickly. Soon Ross pulled onto a dirt road, and then after driving a couple of miles, he turned into a drive that had a gate. He got out of the truck, leaving the door open, and swung the gate to the right. He drove the truck through and closed the gate behind us. We continued along a much rougher driveway toward a green mountain.

At an old barn, he stopped and turned off the engine. "We're here."

I didn't see a house. Or people.

"It's pretty isolated," I observed.

"Boy, you really do have trust issues, don't you?"

I shrugged and opened the door. "I read a lot of true crime, too."

He laughed and reached into the back seat. He handed me a helmet. "Your crown, my lady."

I looked at the dirty red globe. "You couldn't even bother to wash it?"

"I did. You should have seen it *before* I wiped it down for you."

I walked around the truck and stood behind the trailer. Ross joined me. I slid the helmet over my head and tried to fasten the strap. "Here, let me help you with that," he said. He leaned toward my chin. When his fingers brushed my skin, a jolt shot through me, and I blinked. "Your hair's in the way." He ran his long fingers along the side of my face softly, pushing my hair back so that he could pull the strap tight. Our eyes locked. I held perfectly still and couldn't breathe until he moved away.

My head felt heavy and disoriented—either from the helmet or his touch—I wasn't sure which.

"There you go," he said gruffly. He hopped onto the trailer and slid a ramp off the back. Then he walked the bike down the slope. For someone with a limp, he managed all of this with surprising agility and speed. That bike had to weigh at least five hundred pounds.

"You've done that before," I observed.

"About a thousand times. You ready?" He swung onto the bike in one fluid motion.

I looked at the beast. What was I thinking? Why had I agreed to this? My stomach flopped around inside my belly. "You're sure this is safe?"

"Absolutely. Hop on."

I approached the motorcycle, and putting a hand on his arm for balance, I climbed onto the seat awkwardly and sat behind him. Far behind him, barely touching.

"Put your feet there," he said, pointing at metal pegs sticking out. "And hang onto me."

I followed instructions. I clutched the back of his shirt with my hands.

"You have to wrap your arms around me," he said, "or you're going to fall off."

The thought sent heat to my cheeks. Already, my thighs felt warm where my jeans brushed against his, and now I had to press against his broad back? I hadn't thought this through at all.

He clutched the handlebars, squeezed, and kick-started the engine. The bike roared to life beneath us and rumbled, full of power and energy. That motivated me to clutch his stomach with both arms and pull myself tightly against him.

"Ready?" he yelled.

I nodded against his back.

He released whatever lever held the engine still, and suddenly we began moving forward on the bumpy road. The field raced beside us to the left, and to the right, a line of trees blurred. We followed the road until it climbed onto a narrow trail that went into the woods, shifting left and right, bumping over rocks and roots, jarring my teeth and forcing me to clutch Ross with all my strength. It was thrilling!

After several minutes of this, we came to an ash-based path of what looked like an old railroad bed, no longer in use, the wooden ties and rails removed, and he increased the speed. Trees with fresh spring leaves and giant boulders raced past us.

We came to a clearing, and Ross brought us to a stop at a lookout. A valley of freshly turned Alabama red clay fields spread before us, probably prepared for cotton, soybean, or corn.

"You can stop squeezing now," he said, turning off the engine. "I need to breathe."

"Sorry." I let go and slid back on the seat.

Some of those wild brown curls escaped the bottom of his helmet. He half-turned so he could see my face. "Are you having fun yet?"

"Yes!"

"You don't have to act so surprised."

"I was really nervous about this," I admitted. "But you're a good driver."

"I'm hurt that you would think anything else." He pressed his hands against his heart for a moment. Then he shrugged. "The accident made me cautious, that's all. I have a healthy respect for the damage machines can do to the human body."

His helmet hid the scar on his face, but its presence made itself known. "Is that why you have a scar?" I asked. "You wrecked your dirt bike?"

"God no! My parents would never let me ride if I'd hurt myself this way on the bike! We were in a car accident. A guy driving an SUV ran a red light and plowed into our car, crushing my pelvis and breaking my femur and hip. The scar is from hitting my face on the dash."

"How old were you?"

"Ten. I've had a couple of surgeries, but the doctors think this is about as good as it will ever get."

"Does it hurt?"

"Sometimes, with certain weather, my hip aches a little, but that's it." He shrugged. "Anyhow, that's my story. Now for the real reason I brought you out here." He grinned mischievously.

"Uh oh." I began getting nervous again.

"Are you interested in an adventure?"

He'd built up some of my trust, but still I narrowed my eyes. "What kind of adventure?"

"Treasure hunting."

Treasure? I'd expected a lot of things today, but not this.

"What kind of treasure?" I asked. "Where?"

"So many questions." He flashed that crooked smile at me. "Can't you just be spontaneous and say whether you're in or out?"

Was he serious? "Absolutely not."

"No, you're not in?" he asked.

"No, I can't say until I know what kind of treasure and where."

"Sure you can. Live a little."

I shook my head. "You are maddening, do you know that?"

We stared at each other. I tried to imagine myself being spontaneous—and couldn't.

"The 'where' is here... somewhere on my grandfather's farm," he said after a moment. "There's a cave entrance. I want to find it. I want you to help me look."

"And there's buried treasure inside this cave?"

He chuckled. "No, for people like me, the cave itself is the treasure."

"No thanks, I'm really not interested in caving." The idea of crawling down a hole held zero appeal to me.

"You don't have to," he assured me. "I'll explore the cave with my group. I just want your help finding the location of the cave itself. My grandfather knows it's here because he found it once."

I looked at my watch. "Do you think we have time?"

"Next weekend. It might take us awhile. We have quite a bit of acreage to hike." He made a sweeping motion with his arm toward the surrounding hills. "What do you say?" He gave me a pleading look.

I looked at the acreage in question. It looked like *a lot* of walking. "I don't know…"

"Help a poor crippled guy out. I don't want to do it alone."

"You are *not* a 'poor crippled guy,' so don't play the handicapped card with me." I tapped his arm lightly with my fist. It was solid rock.

He batted his eyes. His eyelashes were incredibly long, and his smile was contagious.

"Okay, yes," I said. "Count me in. I'll help you find the cave."

123 / 110

March 16

On Monday morning, first thing after waking up, I went to the bathroom and weighed in. I didn't like what the scale said. My diet wasn't moving as fast as I wanted. I felt stuck. Ten days had passed, and I'd only lost six pounds on Boot Camp. The first five had vanished within seven days, but then I'd lost just one pound since. What was happening? It wasn't like I'd binged all weekend.

I returned to my room, logged onto the computer, and posted:

Olivia: 5'4", 123 / 110: I think I've hit my first plateau since joining the program. Help! What do I do? There are only six weeks until the prom, and I have to meet my goal before then.

I changed into my sweats, stretched, and waited a few minutes to see if anyone else posted a response. Nothing.

I went outside. Instead of my usual number of hill sprints this morning, I vowed to run double: sixteen. Also, a two-mile cool-down, and no breakfast. I didn't deserve it.

By the time I finished the last hill, my legs screamed in pain. Good. No pain, no gain—and hopefully a loss on the scale tomorrow. I glanced at my watch to make sure I had enough time to run two miles and still take a shower before school. I did if I hurried.

Back in my room, there were some posts in response to my plea for help.

Jane: 5'4", 110 / 100: Don't give up, Olivia! You can do it.

Lauren: 5'3.5", 113 / 105: Break through a plateau by shaking things up. If you've been running, try swimming laps. If you've been doing the Boot Camp diet, switch to the raw veggies diet for a week. Anything to confuse your body and give it a new kick-start.

Ana Marie: 5'10", 118 / 120: Lauren's right. Change is the key. Make sure you're not starving yourself, which just makes the body hold onto fat. Eat a little, but switch it up.

Eating didn't make sense. If I starved, wouldn't I lose weight faster? On the other hand, I knew I needed energy to run, and I had a track meet tonight. I needed to win.

So I allowed myself a container of light yogurt for breakfast, rather than a hard-boiled egg, and substituted an apple for my regular banana. Maybe those variations would fool my body.

As far as changing exercise, running was all I knew and wanted to do. Running *more* was the only change to introduce. More, more, more.

At school, I went to my locker after first period with the hope that Brody might visit me again, and he didn't disappoint.

"Hey, Olivia. What's up?"

I clutched my books against my chest and lifted my chin to look at him. "Not much. What about you?"

"I've been thinking about something since I last saw you."

He was thinking about me?

"Oh yeah?" I asked. "What's that?"

He cocked his head to the side and gave me a half smile. "Maybe we should go out a few times before the prom. You know, to get to know each other better."

"Yeah! That would be great."

He shifted from one foot to the other. "How about Friday night?"

"Sorry, I can't. I work Friday and Saturday nights."

"Oh yeah, where do you work?"

"Grace Lake Diner."

"Waitress?" he asked.

"Dishwasher."

"Oh." He made a face. It wasn't the most glamorous job.

I shrugged and said, "It's a paycheck."

"When are you free, then? You have track practice after school, and I have baseball."

"What about after practice, like Thursday?" I asked.

"Sure, we can meet by the gym."

I nodded. "Okay, then."

He looked at his sports watch. "We'd better go, or we're both going to be late to class."

"We can't have that, or our first date will be in detention together," I joked.

He gave me a sideways smile, flashing those dimples, and then he took a step backwards, turned, and walked away. I scurried in the opposite direction and slid into my seat just as the bell rang.

I thought about the conversation with Brody. What had changed since he last saw me that made him decide to ask me out? The thing that kept coming up in my mind was that I'd told him how much weight I'd lost. Could five pounds really make such a big difference? And if so, what would happen after I lost *nineteen* pounds?

122 / 110

March 19

At lunch on Thursday, Alice and Nash went especially overboard with their "lovey bunches" and their public displays of affection because it was their anniversary. Three years together. Nash gave Alice a pair of amethyst earrings, her birthstone. She gave him a new tattoo, or at least planned to pay for him to add one to the collection of body art he'd already amassed.

I nibbled on carrot sticks—a feeble attempt to shake up my diet—and watched them feed one another with potato chips. What was that like—to be cared for by another person, to be fed?

"Why the frowny face, Olivia?" Nash asked.

"Was I frowning?"

"More of a scowl, I think," Alice said. "Like this." She scrunched her brow together and puckered her lips.

"No, I wasn't!"

"Are you nervous about your date with Brody?" she asked.

I sagged into the table. "Yeah, kind of."

"Do you know where he's taking you?" She lazily pulled apart the crust of her pizza without eating it. All she was doing was shredding the pieces. I loved pizza crust. I couldn't believe she could just leave it on her tray like that, like it was no big deal. The crust was the best part.

"No. All I know is that we're meeting here after practice tonight." I shoved a carrot stick into my mouth.

"Just relax and be yourself. He's into you."

Their advice was impossible to follow. I felt nervous all afternoon. At track practice, I channeled that energy into my running, which made Coach Wilby happy. Afterwards, I hurried to the showers to get ready for the date.

When I emerged from the locker room, Brody was already leaning against one of the vending machines beside the side door of the school. Baseball practice had ended earlier than ours. He gave me a slow, easy smile and nodded.

"That works," he said.

"For what?" I wasn't sure what he was talking about, but I thought he might be referring to my choice of clothing. Since he hadn't mentioned where we were going, I'd decided to wear something versatile: khakis and a white blouse with flats.

"Mini golf."

"Sounds fun!" I reached his side. He took my hand. I gulped and followed him to his car, as if holding hands with Brody Tipton was the most natural thing in the world.

He drove us to the Family Fun Center in town. They had mini golf, go-carts, bumper cars, and a bunch of arcade games. Thursday night wasn't too crowded, but the weekends could be brutal at this place. I stood aside while he went to the counter and bought our tickets. The smell of popcorn and burgers filled the air. My stomach growled loudly. It was dinnertime but no food for me. I refused to eat any of the junk here.

"If you don't mind," I said to Brody when he returned, "I want to get a drink before we start. I'm really thirsty from practice."

"I'll get it for you. What do you want?"

"That's okay. You don't have to."

"My treat." His blue eyes insisted.

"Diet Coke would be great."

"Hold these." Brody handed the tickets to me and went to another counter for the soda. He returned with my drink, a drink for himself, and some of that wonderful smelling popcorn.

"You hungry?" he asked, offering the bucket to me.

"No thanks, this is all I want." I took a big gulp through the straw before my stomach could growl and contradict me again.

"Let's sit down somewhere and finish this first."

We went to an empty table near the bumper car arena. Screaming children ran gleefully around us, and arcade machines made all sorts of computer noises. I leaned forward, grinning.

"It's a carnival in here, isn't it?" I said.

"All day, every day. I bring my little sister here a lot."

"I didn't know you had one. How old is she?"

"Eight."

I tried to picture Brody hanging out with a blonde eight-year-old girl with pigtails. "I bet she adores her big brother."

He gave me one of those dimpled grins. "I'm pretty much Superman in her book."

"What's her favorite thing here?"

"Go-carts, hands down."

"So why are we doing mini golf tonight instead of go-carts?"

"Because go-carts are not a first date event," he said. "They're at least a level 3."

"Really?" I giggled. "I think I'm up for the challenge."

His eyes danced. "You say that now, but you haven't even played a game of mini golf with me yet. Come on, are you ready?"

I slurped the last of my Diet Coke. "Ready!"

We stood, and I followed Brody outside to the putt-putt course. He exchanged our tickets for two clubs and golf balls.

"Ladies first," he said, sweeping his arm forward.

"Why thank you," I said. He was being as sweet to me as Nash was with Alice. I smiled and moved to the first hole. "I have to warn you, I'm no good at this game."

"Sounds like a hustler to me. Are you trying to get me to place a wager on our match?"

"I don't gamble," I said.

"One goodnight kiss if I win, and two if you win," he suggested.

Oh, my. I gulped and managed to say, "You'll let me win."

He chuckled. "You're assuming I want to kiss you."

I blushed, lowered my head, and focused on trying to hit the ball. I gave it a whack, and the ball went flying in a direction nowhere near the hole.

When I straightened, I discovered that Brody had come up right behind me and placed a hand on my hip. It burned where his fingers rested. He lowered his voice. "I *do* want to kiss you," he said. "And you're making it very difficult for me to let you win."

My jaw dropped open, then closed. "You've never liked an easy win," I said, "not as long as I've known you."

He eyed me with appreciation. "You're right."

I stepped away from him and went to my errant ball. I lined up the shot and made the hole.

He smirked, walked up to the starting spot, and made his own shot. Over the next hour, we negotiated the course with the same competitiveness that we'd always shown on the cross country trail. I'd pull ahead, and then he'd pass. He made jokes. I relaxed. We laughed so hard that the family in front of us gave us dirty looks a couple of times.

Things became serious as we approached the last hole, and by coincidence or planning on Brody's part, we were tied.

"It all comes down to this," he said. "One kiss or two."

I'd been having so much fun that I felt reckless in my flirting. "Or, here's a thought," I said. "Kiss me right now, and then we can play for a true win, not a stacked wager."

Brody took a step toward me and leaned on his putter. "An excellent suggestion, Olivia."

"Thank you, it just came to me."

"Eliminate all this distracting tension."

"Um, yeah." I nodded.

"Hold this." He handed his putter to me.

Confused, I took it. He put his hand to the back of my head and lowered his face toward mine. I was so surprised that I didn't move. His lips brushed against mine, softly, and then his mouth opened and pressed into me.

I'd been kissed before. But I'd never had my head locked in someone's hand while his lips did amazing things to mine, rendering me helpless while he explored my mouth, until the couple behind us in the mini golf course cleared their throats and asked us to hurry up so we could all go home.

Brody released me. Dazed, I stumbled.

He took his putter from me. He made the hole in two shots. He walked over to retrieve his ball and looked back at me as if to say, "Beat that."

I took a deep breath to calm my trembling and closed my eyes for a moment. I breathed in slowly, then out. I stroked the ball and made the shot. Hole in one.

121 / 110

March 20

I dreamt that Brody and I went to the prom, and we were a real couple, not just together for the dance. He opened the limousine door and placed his hand on the small of my back, the way I'd seen Nash escort Alice into a movie theatre. He bent to kiss my neck. When we danced, I followed his strong lead, and we moved all over the floor like professionals. I felt as light as air—thin and lovely.

When I glanced at him again, I realized Brody had turned into Ross. It had been Ross all along.

I woke up feeling disoriented. Dreams were just dreams; they didn't mean anything. In this case, the reason both boys showed up was that a terrible conflict was brewing. After my hole in one, and two more kisses, Brody asked me out on another date. He wanted to take me to a movie on Sunday afternoon, and without thinking, I'd said yes.

But now that meant telling Ross that I couldn't go searching for the cave with him this weekend after all.

Or, it meant telling Brody that I couldn't go to the movie on Sunday because I had other plans. But doing what?

It was a big mess. What was I thinking?

I rolled out of bed and approached the bathroom scale. Down another pound. Still a long way from my goal weight, though. I needed to buy my dress early while the selection was good, get any necessary alterations, and feel good about the size and fit. That meant reaching one hundred and ten *before* the week of the prom—so I really had much less than six weeks to reach my goal weight.

Today would be a good day. Today I would not eat anything off plan.

I hurried into my sweats and went for my morning sprints before breakfast. As I pushed myself up the hill, I thought about Blubber Busters. Some of the girls on the message boards talked about binging and purging. I hadn't done any of that. Control: I stuck to the plan. If I ate an extra hard-boiled egg or apple, I ran an extra sprint the next morning. I avoided sugar at all costs because the idea of making myself vomit seemed too extreme to contemplate. Exercise was my method for purging. On weekends, I could run ten or twelve miles, if necessary, to work off extra calories consumed during the week.

After working out and eating my single hard-boiled egg, I went to school. I looked forward to seeing Brody at my locker again after first period because he'd become such a frequent visitor these past two weeks, and he didn't disappoint me.

"Hey, Olivia," he said, swiping the underside of my chin with the tip of his finger before slouching against the bank of lockers.

"Hi." I grabbed the books I needed.

"I had fun last night."

"Even though you lost?" I joked.

He lowered his voice and brought his face very close to mine. "I didn't lose."

I thought about the kissing and blushed. Neither of us really lost.

"I guess you need to give me your phone number," he said. "So I know where to pick you up on Sunday."

"Oh! Right!" I flipped my notebook to a blank page and scribbled my number for him. "Here." I shoved the paper at him.

He gave me another one of those slow, half smiles. "I'll call you around two, after you're off work, okay?"

I swallowed and nodded, wondering if he would kiss me again, right here in the middle of the hallway. It was a ridiculous thought because I knew he wouldn't, but I wanted him to.

"See you later," he said.

I watched him saunter away from me with that long, easy stride. I sighed and headed for physics class. We needed to be studying something relevant like magnetic fields or gravitational pull. Those were the forces acting upon my body at that moment.

In Spanish class, we had a test, so I didn't have a chance to talk with Alice about the date with Brody until lunch, when we met up with Nash.

"It was wonderful," I simply said to both of them, peeling my banana.

Alice rolled her eyes toward the ceiling. "We want details. Was there kissing?"

"Was there tongue?" Nash added.

"I am *not* answering that question!"

"Oh, my!" they said in unison.

"Tongue on the first date!" Nash said.

"This is serious," Alice observed. "Where did he take you?"

"To the Family Fun Center, of all things. We played mini golf." I grinned. "We had the best time together. Lots of flirting."

"Was the kissing at the golf center itself, or later?"

Hmm. Both. I took a bite from my banana and took my time swallowing. I was absolutely not giving details of last night's kissing wager to these two. They'd spend the entire lunch hour dissecting the meaning behind the whole thing.

"He asked me out again," I offered at last.

"Already? When?" Alice asked.

"Sunday. We're going to a movie."

"See, I told you he was into you," Nash said.

I smiled, thinking about everything that happened last night, as well as the way Brody had looked at me this morning in front of the lockers. "Yeah, I think he is, too."

"And I can tell you're into him, too," Alice said. "You've fallen big time."

I thought about my dream and the way everything was going—right up until the point when Brody turned into Ross. I thought falling in love meant that my thoughts would be consumed by *one* guy, not two. I expected clarity instead of confusion.

At Grace Lake Diner that night, Sally was training Ross for the main cook job so that he could take more shifts over summer until college started in the fall, and that meant that she ran him ragged throughout the night.

I knew I'd make more money as a waitress and that I ought to train to take one of those shifts in the summer, too. It would help with costs for books and other college fees. The idea terrified me, though. What if I messed up the orders? What if I dropped the food? What if people didn't like me? Here in the kitchen, behind the scenes, I knew I could do a good job. Out in the dining room in the public spotlight, there were too many variables.

Telling Ross that I couldn't go caving with him because of my date with Brody seemed easy when I was looking into Brody's blue eyes and dimples and nodding, but now, it seemed harder. Brody might be "the one," but Ross was already my friend. I didn't want to hurt his feelings, and I didn't know how to be honest without doing that.

I watched him limp from the cooler to the grill. It was just a small hitch in his gait, something I hardly noticed at all now that I knew him better. As if sensing my gaze, he looked up and smiled. I smiled back and fanned my face as if to say, "It's hot in here." He nodded in agreement.

The thing about kitchen work was that there was always something that needed to be done. Once I caught up with the dining room dishes, I went over to the basin and began washing the cook's pots. I never finished everything until the place closed.

Ross came up behind me and reached into the clean side for a stirring spoon. "Sally's killing me," he whispered.

"You asked to be a grill cook. This torture is your own choice."

"Oh yeah." He grinned. The humidity made his wild curls stick out even more than usual.

"You'd better stop talking to me and go back over there before she fires you," I said.

Sally poked her head around the corner of the steam table. I plunged my hands into the soapy water and turned away from him.

"Ross, get your butt over here!" she barked. "You want these burgers to burn into charcoal?"

He scurried over to the grill. Hot fat sizzled and spat. I shook my head and grinned to myself. There was no way I'd ever volunteer to work Sally's kitchen. That boy was nuts.

At the end of our shift, when Ross and I carried the garbage out to the dumpster together, I decided to come clean with him about Brody. Our friendship would probably end over this, but I felt that I had to tell the truth.

"I have some bad news," I began. "I can't go with you on Sunday to look for that cave."

"Oh no, why not?"

I scrunched up my face. "I'm sort of seeing this guy."

"Sort of?" His deep voice took on a wary tone.

"The day before I met you, he'd just asked me out to the prom. That's it. But now we've started *dating* dating, and…" I shrugged. "I like him."

"And he asked you out on Sunday."

"Yeah. I'm really sorry."

Ross stared at me for a moment. I felt awful, like there was a lump inside my stomach the size of a grapefruit or something. I wanted to throw up.

"What about next Sunday?" he asked.

"Really?" I couldn't keep the disbelief from my voice.

"Sure, I mean, we're friends. I get it." He threw the garbage bag into the dumpster.

"Yeah, we are," I said. "I want to help you find that cave. And I'd like to keep hanging out."

"Okay, we will." He headed back toward the restaurant. I followed.

He stayed quiet, though, and wouldn't meet my eyes while we finished cleaning up. When it came time to part ways in the parking lot, he hurried to his car after a quick goodbye. Usually we stood around and talked for a few minutes.

Maybe he'd changed his mind and didn't want to hang out after all.

I wouldn't blame him. I decided to let him think about it, and if he came back and wanted to end our friendship or withdraw his Sunday invitation, I'd give him a way to get out of it gracefully. I understood. He'd been caught off guard and put on the spot.

I felt bad about the whole thing.

At home after taking a shower, I ate my usual dinner. It had been a good day on plan: one hard-boiled egg, one banana, and one can of light chicken noodle soup. I heated the soup for two minutes in the microwave and then ate it slowly, following a ritual I had developed during my diet. I ate the carrots first. One carrot nibble at a time. Then the green beans—one at a time. Then the other vegetables. I spooned the broth, which by this time was lukewarm at best. At the very end, I ate one noodle at a time, and finally, the chicken. Eating my dinner this way took fifteen minutes, sometimes twenty. I ate without television or reading material, concentrating completely on the food. I'd been thinking about the food all day. I was very, very hungry. I was always hungry now. And cold.

After eating the soup, I drank a very large glass of water. Then I logged onto the computer and checked the Blubber Busters message boards for awhile. Reading some of the posts made me begin feeling really fat and bad about myself. They made every unwanted bulge on my body feel hot and throbbing, like something that needed to be sliced off with a razor blade. That stubborn roll around my waist. That pucker between my hip and upper thigh when I sat a certain way. That bit of fat on the back of my upper arm. Cut it all off.

These thoughts felt black and dangerous. Part of me understood that I felt bad because of what happened with Ross tonight, but the other part felt certain that I needed to punish myself for hurting him. I should never have agreed to hang out with him in the first place, even though I really liked him and his taste in books and music and the way he drove that dirt bike around the woods. Or, I should have told him about Brody sooner. I didn't do it last Sunday because I had too much fun, and that was selfish of me. I'd led him to think that things between us were more than they were.

My stomach grumbled, still hungry. The soup wasn't enough. I wrapped myself in blankets and waited for morning.

120 / 110

March 22

After my Sunday breakfast shift at the diner, I went home and showered for my date with Brody. I changed clothes four times before deciding on a pair of tight jeans and a cute sweater top that showed off my new figure. I wanted Brody to see how hard I was working for those prom pictures.

He'd sent me a text to get my address and said he'd pick me up around two-thirty, and now it was time. Something useless played on the television. As always, a candy dish sat in the center of the coffee table, and a pile of empty foils from Hershey's Kisses sat on the table beside Mom's elbow. I sat by the living room window, waiting for his car to round the corner, his name running through my mind like a song. My foot jiggled crazily, waiting.

"You look like you've lost a lot of weight," Mom observed.

Crap, I shouldn't have hung out around her in my skinny jeans.

I shrugged. "A couple of pounds. Not much."

She shook her head. "That's more than a couple of pounds, Olivia. You need to stop that weird diet."

"It's not a weird diet. I'm just eating more protein and healthy foods."

"Where did you find this diet?"

I didn't want Mom to go snooping around the Blubber Busters site. She might misunderstand the posts in some of the groups. There were girls with *really* radical ideas about dieting and weight. "I don't know. It's just fruit, eggs, soup... There's nothing weird about that."

"How much weight have you lost?"

I rolled my eyes and sighed. "I'm about to go on a date with a really cute guy, Mom. I don't need twenty questions about this right now."

"Why are you being so secretive about it?"

"Because you're making a big deal out of nothing. Besides, I'm eighteen now," I reminded her. Graduation was less than three months away. "Adults are allowed to eat whatever they want."

She pursed her lips.

"I'm healthy, and I've never felt better," I said, trying to reassure her. "Don't worry."

"I'm going to worry. You're my daughter. What you're doing isn't healthy—no matter what you say about it."

"Eating all that chocolate isn't healthy, either," I said, looking pointedly at the candy dish.

She glared at me but didn't say anything else. How could she? If we were going to start comparing diets and weight, she was guilty of going down the other extreme path. I hated to say anything like that, but I felt like she'd pushed me into a corner. I wanted her to leave me alone. I wanted her to drop it.

After that, she did.

At last, a car turned into the driveway, and the face behind the wheel was Brody's. I leaped off the chair so fast my mom jumped, startled.

"You bring him inside to say hello," Mom called as I ran to the foyer.

I rolled my eyes. I stopped by the door, breathless, and waited for him to knock. Another eternity passed.

The doorbell rang. I opened the door. Brody stood there, looking tall and blonde and gorgeous. "Come in," I said. "You have to meet the parental unit."

"Which one?" he raised his eyebrows.

"Mom. She's relatively harmless. Come on."

He followed me into the living room.

"Mom, this is Brody Tipton. Brody, my mother."

"Nice to meet you, Mrs. Ingram," Brody said.

"A pleasure, Brody. You kids have a good time at the movies. When are you going to be home?"

"Mom!" I protested, scowling. I shot her a look and mouthed, "Eighteen."

She pointed at the ceiling and mouthed back, "My roof."

"Before ten o'clock," Brody suggested.

Mom raised her eyebrows. "How many movies are you going to see?"

I wanted to die.

"We might grab a bite to eat, too. Maybe play another round of mini golf."

"Mom, please." I gave her a pleading look.

She smiled. "Go, have fun. See you later."

I made a bee-line for the door, hoping that Brody was right on my heels. We needed to exit fast before she asked any other questions.

Outside, I slowed my step in case Brody wanted to open the car door for me the way that Nash did for Alice, but he circled around to the driver's side and got in without waiting for me. I opened my own door.

"A rematch, huh?" I asked as he backed out of the driveway.

"It seemed like a safe answer. I have no idea what we're going to do after the movie."

"Let's start there," I said.

At the theatre, we stood in front of the ticket counter and tried to figure out what to watch. We settled on the latest superhero action movie. Brody bought tickets for both of us, and then we went inside to consider the concession stand.

"We have to get popcorn," Brody said.

"You can get some if you want."

"You won't eat any?"

"I'm not hungry," I said. "I ate before you came because I wasn't sure."

I'd eaten carrot sticks to help fight cravings because that's one of the suggestions on the Blubber Busters boards. When going somewhere that you'll be faced with temptations, don't go hungry. But carrot sticks were no match for the delicious food smells and the display case of monster-sized chocolate delights.

Brody walked up to the counter and ordered a large bucket of popcorn with butter, regular Coke, and Peanut M&Ms—also one of my favorite kinds of candy.

He handed the M&Ms to me to carry.

"You look great," he said. "I can tell you've lost a lot of weight in the past few weeks."

I shrugged, as though it wasn't such a big deal. "A few pounds, I guess." Pride at my accomplishment surged. "Although to be honest, until you said something that day, I didn't realize there was anything wrong with the way I looked."

He stopped and looked at me. "Olivia, I'm sorry if you took it that way. I didn't mean that you looked *bad*. I just meant that you could look *better*. And you do already, even with the few pounds that you've lost."

I blinked, stung by his words, which implied that he thought I could look *even better* if I lost more—which I intended to do, but which I also didn't necessarily want him to point out. I'd wanted him to be thrilled with me now, already.

"Don't worry," I said, just to confirm my suspicion, "by prom night, I'll be so skinny you'll hardly recognize me."

"I know you will. I've seen the way you train for cross country. You can do anything you set your mind to." He popped a handful of popcorn into his mouth. "You ready to go inside?"

"Yeah." I swallowed the lump in my throat.

In the theatre, I handed the M&Ms to him. Even though I'd eaten those carrot sticks, the buttery smell of the popcorn tortured me. It took every ounce of willpower to stop my hand from plunging into the bucket and gorging myself. I wanted to cry. How could he be so cruel, especially if he knew I was dieting and trying to lose weight for him?

He's oblivious, I told myself. It's nothing to him. As he'd said earlier, he believed in me so much that he thought it was no big deal for me to sit here while he ate, and besides, I'd told him that I wasn't hungry. Why would he think anything was wrong?

I couldn't enjoy the movie, even though I loved superhero movies, and especially this one.

"What do you want to do now?" he asked when the movie was over. "I thought about dinner somewhere, but after eating that popcorn, I'm not really hungry, are you?"

What was I supposed to say? *Take me somewhere I could get a salad while you watch me eat.* No way.

"Do you like coffee?" I asked. "We could go somewhere and get coffee and talk for awhile."

"Sure, okay."

We returned to his car and drove to a nearby bookstore that had a café area.

"My treat, since I suggested it," I said.

I ordered mine black, and he ordered a frothy caramel one. We found two oversized chairs in the corner and settled in. My eyes feasted on the rows of bookcases surrounding us, and I thought about the wonderful conversation that Ross and I had had last weekend about our favorite authors and books.

"What do you like to read?" I asked. "When you come to a bookstore like this, where do you browse?"

"I never go to bookstores."

"Oh." I sipped my coffee. "Never?"

"I don't like to read."

"Oh, okay." End of that thread. I could offer my favorite books, but I didn't think we'd get very far with that.

He looked bored already. I went for a subject that I knew would hold his attention. "So how's baseball going?"

That lit him up. He talked for a good twenty minutes about his favorite sport. I nodded and listened, although baseball interested me about as much as books interested him.

After finishing our coffee and exhausting the subject of America's pastime, Brody asked, "Now what?"

"Home, I think. It's a school night, after all."

He made a pouty face.

"I know, I hate Mondays, too." I stood.

I threw my trash into the bin, and Brody followed. He took my hand as we walked through the store to the doors.

At the car, he released my hand and walked around to the driver's side. I sat and reached for my seat belt. He stopped me with his hand on mine.

"What?" I asked, puzzled.

He reached up and brushed my hair with feather-soft fingers. His blue eyes gazed into mine for a long moment, and then he leaned forward and kissed me. Warmth spread slowly through my limbs, and I tentatively pressed toward him in return. His arms wound around my back, clutching me toward him, the console rising up between us like a barrier, and his hands caressed my shoulders. The kiss began to deepen as his tongue explored mine.

As his passion grew stronger, more insisting and rough, my own suddenly cooled. I continued to allow him to hold me, but I couldn't continue responding to kisses that felt more like an invasion than an invitation.

"What's wrong?" Brody asked.

I shrugged. "A bit too much, too fast," I admitted.

Brody sat back in his seat and sighed. "You're one of those."

"One of what?"

He closed his eyes and frowned for a moment like he was in pain or something. I wasn't sure what to think. I suddenly just wanted to end the date and go home.

"How many serious boyfriends have you had?" he asked.

How did he define "serious"? Regardless, the answer to the question was easy for me. "None."

"None, really?"

I blushed. "I don't think many guys see me as girlfriend material. I'm a jock and a nerd."

"I can see why you might get overlooked," he agreed. "In school, that's how you portray yourself, too. You don't dress to show yourself off."

"I never wanted that kind of attention."

"You should, though. You could be so hot."

I stared at my hands in my lap. *Could be.* To Brody, I seemed to be very incomplete.

"Why did you even ask me out?" I asked. "You don't seem to really like me the way I am."

"I've liked you since cross country. I wouldn't be here if I didn't. I'm just saying that I see potential for you to better yourself."

I felt tears stinging in my throat.

He took my hand. "You're taking this the wrong way. I think you're great. You said you're not one of those showy girls at school, and I know, I get that. Okay. But what I see is that you're one of those girls with low self-confidence who doesn't realize how pretty she really is. I just wanted to help you see that."

I gave him a sideways glance. I wasn't sure what to think about him. A very tiny part of me urged caution; the buttered popcorn, the hurtful comments, and the pushy kisses resonated a lot with the warnings that Tammy had given me about him. *Be careful*.

On the other hand, he hadn't *really* said or done anything that wasn't typical guy-like behavior, had he? Didn't everyone make insensitive comments or do careless things once in awhile? And what teenage boy didn't try to push his kisses as far as possible, as fast as possible?

He'd said that he thought I was pretty and that he wanted me to meet my full potential. That sounded like a nice thing. And at the end of the date, the most important thing was that gorgeous Brody Tipton had chosen me. I wanted to be worthy.

At home that night, I couldn't stand it anymore. I snuck into the kitchen and opened the pantry. I grabbed the jar of peanut butter, the package of chocolate chips, the loaf of bread, and a spoon. First I made plain peanut butter and bread sandwiches and ate three of those. Then I ate spoonfuls of peanut butter with chocolate chips pressed on top. By the time I finished, more than half the bag of chips and most of the peanut butter was gone. I felt bloated, weak, and disgusted with myself. It was my first binge since starting Blubber Busters.

I thought about the girls who purged when something like this happened. If I logged in and asked for help, many would suggest that route.

But I didn't want to do that. It was a line I didn't want to cross. If I lost weight by reducing my calories on a normal meal plan, then I was just dieting. If I started binging and purging, then I had an eating disorder.

That wasn't me.

120 / 110

March 24

On Tuesday morning, I stepped on the scale hopefully, but the numbers refused to budge. I was being punished for my binge on Sunday afternoon.

I'd been weak, but today I renewed my commitment. Back to basics: Boot Camp 101. What worked in the beginning would work again. It would be a good day.

After logging my weight into my Blubber Busters profile, I browsed a few posts on the boards.

Jane: 5'4", 109 / 100: Feeling low this morning.

Olivia: 5'4", 120 / 110: What's wrong, Jane?

Jane: 5'4", 109 / 100: I binged last night and feel awful. Bloated, weak, defeated.

Olivia: 5'4", 120 / 110: You're not alone. It's one blip. Look ahead, not behind.

Jane: 5'4", 109 / 100: Some days, I'm just so tired of this.

Olivia: 5'4", 120 / 110: Be kind to yourself, Jane. It's a marathon, not a sprint. Just remember, you are worth it.

Jane: 5'4", 109 / 100: Thanks, Olivia.

I put on my sweats and pulled my hair into a ponytail before heading outside to run sixteen hill strides, followed by a three mile hard run. For breakfast, I ate one hard-boiled egg.

Before Spanish class, Alice and I had a few minutes to talk without Nash around. "When do you want to go dress shopping?" I asked. This date was my true deadline for meeting my goal weight, not May 2nd. I needed to be the correct size by the time I bought my fabulous gown.

"I was just thinking about that last night," she said. "We need to go soon. This weekend is bad, but how about next weekend?"

Next weekend? I wouldn't be ready!

She continued. "We can go in the morning so you don't have to miss work."

"That would be great since I need to work to pay for the dress." I tried to calculate how much weight I could lose in eighteen days. Was it possible to lose ten pounds that fast?

"The weekend after that, I can't go," she continued, "and after that, we're getting too close to the prom. I'm probably going to need alterations on whatever I get, so I want to have some time. April 4th is really the best date."

I nodded, hating it. "Okay, let's shoot for April 4th."

I didn't know how I'd be able to lose weight that fast, but I'd do my best. Once again, that small voice inside of me suggested joining the ranks of other Blubber Busters who starved completely and purged any morsel of food that others forced upon them.

Could I continue to be high-minded about that?

I opened my notebook and tried to pay attention to Mrs. Oren as class started. No, I couldn't cross into that realm. Not me. That wasn't me.

Sunny skies and spring temperatures graced our track meet on Tuesday afternoon. We didn't need our sweats to stand on the sidelines and watch the events. Coach Wilby—hatless, his balding head gleaming in the sun—paced among the athletes like a short drill sergeant. His froggy eyes bulged as he offered encouragement and instructions for upcoming events.

Tammy and I stood at the end of the bleachers and stretched in preparation for the 3200m.

"You look really skinny in that uniform," she said. "How much weight have you lost?"

Nine pounds since March 5th. But advice from the Blubber Busters boards suggested that I should keep actual losses to myself. Numbers caused alarm and interference from well-meaning loved ones.

"I don't know, not that much," I said. "These shirts make everyone look skinny. There's hardly any material at all."

"I can even tell in your face."

I rolled my eyes like she was crazy. "You're imagining things. I can't see any difference in my face."

Coach Wilby walked over to us. "All right, you're up next. Should be no problem taking first and second place with this team. Their best runner's a distant third to you two."

"We're ready," Tammy said. "No worries."

We followed him to the starting line. It was a small group for this event because not many people enjoyed the 3200m. At the starter pistol, Tammy and I immediately took the lead and set the pace for the race. As Coach Wilby suggested, their top runner fell behind after the first lap.

Into the third lap, I began feeling weak and light headed—even slightly dizzy. Tammy, who'd been trying to beat me in a race since sophomore year, pulled ahead of me on the far side of the track. I tried to pick up the pace. I couldn't let her win. I visualized that little horse from my favorite movie, pulling from behind in the final lap, mustering all his energy to pass the entire pack of horses and win the race. Instead, the runner from the other team came barreling from behind me and passed me on the last curve.

I placed third.

Gasping, I doubled over at the finish line and hoped the nausea would pass.

Tammy came over to me, grinning at first because of her victory, and then giving me a look of concern. "Are you all right?" she asked. "What happened?"

I put my hand on her shoulder. "Congratulations. You finally beat me."

"No." She shook her head. "That wasn't your best effort. What's wrong?"

Coach Wilby reached our side. "What was that all about, Olivia?"

"I don't know," I said. "I'm not feeling well."

He looked concerned. "Does anything in particular hurt?"

"No, I'm just sick to my stomach. Maybe it's a bug or something."

I went to the side of the track and sat on the asphalt. I didn't want them to know how dizzy I felt, and I certainly didn't want to faint. The truth was that I hadn't eaten anything other than my hard-boiled egg today. No banana at lunch because Alice and I were going dress shopping in less than two weeks. That's probably what was wrong.

"Olivia?" A familiar voice. I looked up into the glare of sunlight.

The man had tousled brown hair, the faint stubble of a beard, and brown eyes that looked concerned as they gazed down at me.

"Julian?"

"What happened out there?" my big brother asked.

I jumped to my feet and threw my arms around his neck, grateful that he was strong because my head immediately began spinning crazily again.

"What are you doing here?" I exclaimed.

"Spring break. I thought I'd surprise you."

My humiliating performance on the track slammed into me. Not only had I just *lost*, but I'd lost in front of Julian.

"I'm definitely surprised," I said. "You could have warned me."

"Wow, you've lost a lot of weight."

I released him and took two steps backward. "Not really."

"I can feel your ribs."

"You can feel everyone's ribs when their arms are raised like that."

He gave me a funny look. "If you say so." He looked at the track and repeated his earlier question. "What happened out there?"

I stared at the ground. "I must have a bug or something because my stomach's upset."

He took a step backward. "And you just rubbed it all over me. Thanks a lot! Now I'm going to be sick on my break."

I put my hands on my hips and rolled my eyes. "It's always about you, isn't it, Julian? Even when *I'm* the one who's sick."

"You're really not feeling well?" He squinted at me.

"No! Do you think I *like* losing? Tammy's never going to let me hear the end of this."

Having Julian at home was a rare treat. Graduate school kept him so busy that he called us infrequently, and in person we could tell how exhausted he was from his studies.

"No girlfriends?" I teased that evening as we played a game of Yahtzee together.

"Nope, you?"

"Girlfriends? Alice is still my BFF. And you met Tammy at the track meet."

"You know what I meant." He threw the dice on board and kicked me with his foot. "Any boyfriends?"

I shrugged. "Sorta kinda."

He raised his eyebrows and smirked. "Oh *really*. Spill it."

"His name is Brody Tipton. He asked me to the prom first, and now we've gone out on a few pre-prom dates."

"Do I know him?"

I watched Julian record his score, and then I picked up the dice and threw them.

"No, I don't think so." Brody hadn't run cross country until sophomore year, after Julian graduated, and there wasn't any other reasons for their paths to cross in school.

Julian grinned. "The prom, huh?"

"I know it's hard to picture me in a dress," I said, picking two sixes and setting them aside before rolling the other dice, "but I'm getting excited about it. I've been looking at gowns online. I've been saving money from my job and should be able to buy something nice."

"My little sister's finally growing up."

"That means *you're* getting really old."

I recorded my score and pushed the dice across the board to Julian. He didn't pick them up. He was having too much fun picking on me.

"Are you going to wear your hair in your signature ponytail?" he asked.

"Very funny."

He smirked.

I crossed my ankles and leaned back on my hands. "I'm going to do something special with it, but I haven't decided yet, smarty pants. Hair styles cannot be decided lightly."

"I wish I could be here to see it."

"Come! The prom's on May 2nd."

He shook his head. "Impossible."

We played a few games of Yahtzee before calling it a night. I took a shower and went to my room. I lay in bed and ran my fingers along my ribs and hip bones, feeling the things that Julian had noticed when he hugged me and wondering how to carry out my routine in front of him the rest of the week while he stayed with us. Tonight, chicken soup for my dinner had probably seemed normal because I'd told everyone I felt sick, but my morning hill sprints and daily hard-boiled eggs would attract his attention.

My brother's opinion mattered to me. I didn't want his disapproval of my diet, and I didn't want to have to explain myself. He'd already made comments about feeling my ribs. I didn't need him to draw Mom's attention to my weight loss again.

On the other hand, I only had eleven days until Alice and I were going dress shopping. How could I possibly reach my goal weight in that amount of time if I didn't follow my diet?

I thought I could probably eat semi-normally for the next two days that Julian planned to stay with us, and after he left, I could make up time by extra running and reduced calorie intake. I definitely wouldn't be able to reach my goal weight by April 4th, but I still had five weeks until the prom. Five weeks to lose ten more pounds.

I could do that.

For a few moments, I allowed myself to think about my performance during the track meet. I couldn't believe I'd taken third place in my event. The feeling of being a complete loser was almost too much to bear because I knew that my loss was my own fault. I couldn't help but remember the way that Erica Miller began losing in races too, as she started getting really skinny. I'd vowed that I'd never let a stupid diet get in the way of my running, and yet, here I was. A loser.

I pressed my hands over the drum-tight skin of my belly. Hunger ached inside there, hollowing me out, making me into the kind of person that everyone said was *so skinny*. Beautiful.

119.5 / 110

March 29

When my Sunday breakfast shift at the diner finally ended, Ross was waiting for me at the counter. An empty plate with a few pie crust crumbs and a coffee cup rested at his elbow. Mrs. Lee made fabulous pies. Behind the counter, an entire cooler displayed her lemon meringue, banana crème, Dutch apple, chocolate crème, strawberry, blueberry, and cherry pies—all baked fresh every morning at five a.m. Before the prom and Blubber Busters and my diet, I used to eat a slice of strawberry pie at the end of every shift. It was my treat to myself for working hard.

Julian's visit had set me back a lot, though. I'd hardly lost anything since last Sunday, and the only reason I hadn't shown a gain was that I'd barely eaten anything since he left Thursday night.

Now I was back on track. No pie for me.

"You ready?" I asked Ross, walking past him and out the door without a backward glance at the display case.

He followed me to the parking lot. I dropped my stuff in the trunk of my car, and he waited for me at the passenger door of the truck. Even though I now knew how to climb into the cab, he opened the door for me and held it until I was safely seated.

One part of me thought: *What a gentleman.*

The other part wondered if he was just checking me out.

Hmm. Maybe both.

After he cranked the diesel engine to life, I asked, "Why the giant tires, anyway?"

"My brother's truck, not mine." He threw the transmission into reverse and backed out of the parking lot.

I bet Brody doesn't know how to back up a truck with a trailer attached.

Where did that thought come from? I shoved it firmly away. No thinking about Brody today.

I'd been looking forward to this hike all weekend. I'd had so much fun the last time I rode on Ross's dirt bike, and I had to admit to great curiosity about this "hidden treasure" that we were searching for.

"So tell me about spelunking," I said. I thought he'd be impressed that I knew this special word for caving.

Instead he gave me a sideways look and said, "We prefer to be called 'cavers.'"

I giggled. "Oh, sorry, tell me about *caving.*"

He smiled, too. "What do you want to know?"

I liked the deep timbre of his voice. Its tone had seemed so unusual, almost jarring at first, when placed with his young face, but now that I knew Ross, I couldn't imagine him sounding any other way. I studied the scar, shaped like a question mark, that ran along the hairline on the right side of his face. So many questions… but we were talking about caving, right? "What do you like about it?" I asked.

He looked at the road and drove with an easy confidence. "Exploring, seeing something that very few people have ever seen before or will ever get to see. There's such a thrill after all the planning, hiking, climbing, walking, crawling… sometimes swimming… to finally see the most awesome stalactites and stalagmites imaginable."

"Swimming?" My insides clenched at the claustrophobic thought of being trapped in a tiny space underground—in water.

"Caves are formed by running water, and since many caves are still active, the water is still in the cave."

I thought about underground rivers hollowing out the solid rock beneath the ground. Sinkholes opened up occasionally around here, sometimes in inconvenient places like the middle of interstate highways.

"Is caving dangerous?" I asked.

"Oh yeah. Especially if you don't know what you're doing. Most accidents happen when someone inexperienced visits a cave alone. I always go with a caving group, and we always have a guide who's been through the cave before."

I bit my lip. "Are there bats?"

"Yes, and snakes, spiders, salamanders, and other animals. I've even seen blind, albino fish in caves before."

"Really!" I tried to imagine such a creature.

He nodded and glanced over at me.

"So if you're not supposed to go into a cave without a group or guide, what are we going to do when we find this cave we're looking for?" I asked.

"Mark the GPS coordinates so that I can bring my group back. We have an experienced caver who does exploration and mapping of new caves, and we'll plan some trips with him to chart the cave. Or, he might be able to find some existing information about the cave once we locate it."

"You're sure there's a cave?"

"You doubt me?"

"I'm just questioning your sources," I said.

"It's a little late now, don't you think? I've got you in the truck."

I swallowed. True enough.

"Relax," Ross said. "My grandfather says that he's been inside. The entrance is big enough that you can crawl into it."

"How far did he go?"

"Not very far. The passage gets narrow quickly, and he was a kid looking into a scary dark place. He didn't explore too far."

We reached the farm. Ross unloaded the dirt bike from the trailer. This time, when he offered to help me with my helmet, I pulled my own hair away from my face and tried to breathe normally while he stood so close to me, looking down at my face, his fingers brushing against my skin.

What was *wrong* with me?

Once we were both helmeted up, he climbed onto the bike, and I swung onto the seat behind him. I abandoned my shyness and slid close, wrapping my arms around his middle in anticipation. I ignored all the forbidden feelings that this closeness caused and hoped he didn't sense anything. I had a boyfriend now, sort of, and Ross and I were just friends.

The bike roared to life beneath us. As we took off, I grinned and pressed my face into the back of his shirt. He smelled like clean fluffy towels.

We raced up the hill and into the woods. The trail twisted back and forth, and I clung tightly to avoid getting thrown off the back. My teeth bounced together. Ross took a different trail from the one we'd used previously. We headed toward the green mountain—and hopefully, the cave.

By the time we reached a stopping place, my cheeks ached from smiling so much. Riding the dirt bike was so much fun! Mud covered my jeans up to my knees because we'd ridden through two small creeks, and I didn't even care.

Ross shut off the engine. "You ready to walk?"

I nodded and loosened the strap on my helmet. "Lead the way."

Ross removed a small pack that he'd tied to the back of the seat. He slung it over his shoulders, and then we left the bike and began hiking up the hill. Because it was spring, many plants hadn't opened their leaves yet, and the underbrush wasn't too thick. A few vines tangled around my ankles every now and then, tripping my feet, but for the most part, we made good progress.

"Do you know where we're going and how to keep from getting lost?" I asked after we'd walked about ten minutes.

He held up a compass.

"Do you know how to use one of those things?"

He held up a GPS.

"Did you think to bring water?"

He tapped the strap of the pack hanging between his shoulders and tapped the side of his head with his index finger. Smart boy.

"Okay, I feel better now." I grinned.

We hiked for three hours, navigating around boulders and fallen trees, and Ross talked about some of his favorite caving expeditions. His passion for his sport was evident in the tone of his voice as he described his adventures. As we walked and talked, I couldn't help but think about all the possible caves beneath our feet with all the unusual formations growing in the limestone. I began to understand the thrill that captured Ross's imagination.

Ross looked at his watch. "I guess we should call it quits and head back. We'll try another area next time."

"It's getting late," I agreed. "And we still have to go back to the bike."

"It's close. We've just been making a big loop, see?" He showed me the GPS.

I was totally lost. I wouldn't have been able to get myself out of the woods to save my own life. "Great, I'll follow you," I said.

He returned us to the bike in no time. It was hot, and we decided to take a break and finish our water bottles before putting on our helmets. I leaned against a tree.

"I'm bummed that we didn't find it," I admitted. "All that walking and no reward."

"A good quest is not without its obstacles."

"I want instant gratification."

"The cave will be worth it. When we find it, you'll be so amazed that you'll forgive all the hours of empty wandering around in the woods."

"It's not empty wandering," I protested. "It's beautiful out here."

"Yeah, it is, isn't it?"

"Some of those rock formations we saw on the north side of the hill were really neat. I can't believe the cave wasn't there. It *belonged* there."

"I know what you mean." He tilted his head and drained the rest of his bottle. "You ready, too?"

I nodded and handed my empty to him. He packed both of them, and we climbed onto the bike. The ride back to the truck was just as thrilling as the one that brought us out here.

When we reached the truck and I took my helmet off, Ross laughed. "You look like a raccoon." He shook his head. "There's mud all over your face, except around your eyes. How did you do that?"

"It's your driving," I complained. "You run through every mud hole that you see."

"Do *I* have mud all over my face?" He smirked. His hazel eyes sparkled with mirth.

He did not.

We loaded the bike onto the trailer and fastened it down with yellow straps. Once it was secure, he opened the door for me.

"Shouldn't I sit on a blanket or something?" I asked. "I'm filthy."

"No, I'll clean it up after we get back. Don't worry about it. Get in."

He stood beside me while I climbed onto the running board. My muddy shoe slipped on the shiny surface, and he was there to catch me. "Easy, I got you," he said.

"Thanks."

Once I sat down, he closed the door and circled to the other side.

"That was a lot of fun," I said as we headed out. "I'm glad you invited me. I wish we'd found it, though."

"Next time. Will you go again?"

"Yeah, I'd like that a lot."

"Sunday?"

I nodded.

"You look cute in all that mud." He chuckled.

That chuckle and the deep timbre of his voice did something inside me. I blushed. I'd loved spending the day with him, and if I were honest with myself, I'd had more fun today than on my last date with Brody. But I wanted to be sure Ross remembered where things stood so there wasn't any confusion.

"Ross… don't say stuff like that."

"It's true."

I bit my lip, then said, "Next Saturday, I'm going shopping with my best friend, Alice, for prom dresses."

He didn't miss a beat. "I'm surprised that you haven't bought yours already."

His response wasn't what I'd expected. "I wanted to be a smaller size before I bought mine," I confessed.

"Why?" He turned his gaze from the road to give me a stern look. "You look great already."

I squirmed. I didn't know what to do with his compliments.

"It's a girl thing. You know…" I closed my eyes and repeated the words that Brody had said to me. "Slim down and fit into a perfect prom dress that's two sizes smaller than my normal size and spend thousands of dollars on pictures of myself in it."

He gave me a funny look. "That doesn't really sound like your kind of thing."

I swiveled my head to look at him, shocked. "Why would you say that? You don't even know me that well."

He pounded a fist against his chest dramatically and sighed. "That hurts me, Olivia. It hurts my heart."

"You've known me *a couple of weeks*. You're in no position to be a judge of my character."

"I'm an observer of people. I pay attention to the details. And based on what I've seen of you at the diner and out here, you don't strike me as the girly-girl type. I mean, I'm sure you're going to look awesome in your prom dress, whatever you buy, but you're not one of those girls who lives for the photo shoot. I've met girls like that."

I had to ask. "And what are those girls like?"

"They do not ride dirt bikes through the woods and get mud caked in their hair. Not ever."

I laughed. "So they're no fun?"

"Absolutely not," he agreed.

"Maybe you'd think differently if you saw me at school," I said. "Maybe the person I am at work isn't the real me."

"Given all the posing and posturing that goes on at your average high school, I'm willing to bet that I see more of the real you at Grace Lake Diner than most people see at your school." He pulled his eyes away from the road to look at me again. He raised his eyebrows.

"You're right about me," I confessed after a moment. "I'm a lot more comfortable in sweats and a ponytail than heels and mascara."

"By the way, you have helmet hair."

"I don't care," I said. "And anyway, so do you."

"See, I knew you'd say that. So don't say I don't know you."

I laughed.

"So for you," he said, "I take it that going to the prom is more about this guy you're seeing than the big event?"

I thought carefully about my answer. My initial response would have been that I'd been thrilled to be asked out by *Brody Tipton*, who I'd had a crush on since the fall, so it was about the guy rather than the event. And I'd started the Blubber Busters diet because of his comments about losing weight, which is something I never would have done on my own.

"Both," I said. "Going with Brody is special. But the prom itself is special because it's the big senior ball before we all graduate and go our separate ways. Missing the prom would be a huge disappointment." I paused, thinking about how hard I'd worked to lose those first ten pounds. "Even though I'm not particularly a girly-girl, I *do* want a chance to wear an elegant gown and go dancing with a guy in a tux for a night. It sounds very romantic."

"Romantic?"

"Yeah, I think that's what I really want: romance."

"Hopefully your boyfriend won't disappoint, then." He made a sour face.

I refused to think about the less-than-romantic last date with Brody. I wanted to believe that the prom would be more like our first date—where we flirted through the entire mini golf game and then had sweet kissing. I pictured an unforgettable dress, dancing, flirting, kissing... a bit of romance. By then, maybe even true love.

118 / 110

March 30

On Monday morning, I woke up from a dream with Ross. We'd been searching the woods for the cave. He'd been telling stories and making me laugh and holding my hand, and my mood when the alarm went off was light.

I went to the bathroom to step on the scale. Although Julian's visit had set me back by a week, returning to my boot camp fundamentals had made the number move in the right direction again. Thank goodness! Maybe my break would shake things up enough that I wouldn't have another one of those dreaded plateaus before the prom.

If I lost one pound per day, I could still be one hundred and fourteen by Saturday.

I didn't think that was possible, but that would be ideal. Maybe I could do it if I ran ten miles a day and didn't eat anything at all.

As had become my custom, I returned to my room, logged onto the computer, and posted:

Olivia: 5'4", 118 / 110: A good day today. I'm feeling strong again and past my plateau. Thanks to everyone for the support. These boards are great.

I looked for Jane in the posts. She'd been discouraged lately, and I'd been trying to cheer her up. She was down a half pound this morning.

Olivia: 5'4", 118 / 110: Hey Jane, looks like you finally broke through that plateau. Great job!

I put on my sweats and stretched a few minutes before heading downstairs. Mom wasn't awake yet, and the house was dark and quiet. I loved this time of the day. Everything seemed possible.

Today would be a good day. Today I would stay on plan. Today I would win.

Outside, it was sprinkling. The air smelled like spring. I went back inside to grab my rain jacket and then headed down the driveway. My legs felt tight after all that hiking with Ross yesterday, so I stretched my calves and quadriceps one more time beside the mailbox before walking to the bottom of the hill. Blood pulsed through my veins. Taking a few deep breaths, I sprinted to the top, turned, and walked back to the bottom.

Repeat fifteen times.

Our cross country course had one of the worst hills in the school district. Everyone hated to compete against us on our home trail because the hill was legendary. It was long, winding, steep, and rocky. I'd passed many runners walking up the hill because they couldn't make the last part.

Our coach made us run hill sprints on it at least once a week, and everyone on the team could run the entire race without stopping on that hill. It gave us a distinct advantage on home meets, and even on away meets, because no hills compared to that one in length or intensity. If you could run our hill, you could run any hill.

After running my morning sprints in front of the house, I went for a two-mile run to cool down. My legs felt like lead. Ross and I must have covered a lot of ground yesterday, and I didn't realize it because this morning, my muscles ached in new places.

Good! That meant I'd burned a lot of calories yesterday afternoon. I hadn't even thought about the exercise benefits of hanging out with Ross and searching for the cave.

I ate a hard-boiled egg for breakfast.

After first period, Brody met me at the usual place.

"Hey, Olivia." He leaned against the lockers and looked down at me with a dimpled smile that showed off his perfect teeth.

"Hi. Did you have a good weekend?" I blurted out the question before thinking.

"Yeah, I played some baseball. What about you?"

"I worked, mostly." I shifted my books in my arms. I didn't want to tell Brody about my friendship with Ross because it seemed complicated, but I didn't want to lie to him either. I decided on a half-truth. "And on Sunday afternoon, I hung out with a friend from the diner."

"Cool." He tilted his head in such a way that his blonde bangs hung over his brows at an angle. "So… you want to ride go-carts with me tonight?"

I grinned. "You mean I've moved to level 3 already?"

"You have." He pinned me with his intense blue eyes.

"Sure! Meet me at the same time and place?"

"Yeah. See you then."

I slammed my locker shut. A couple of girls walked past me, gave me a look, and then put their heads together, whispering. I couldn't help but wonder if they were talking about me and Brody. It made me feel self-conscious. After all, half the time I wondered why he was dating me, too.

I went to my physics class. Despite distractions and lack of motivation, my grades remained good—all A's and B's. I'd applied to three colleges but hadn't received any acceptance letters yet. No rejections either, but I was eager to finalize my fall plans.

Food was on my mind. Food was always on my mind. I opened my notebook and doodled pictures of cupcakes with frosting and cherries on top. I doodled pies and cakes. I doodled a feast.

On my way to the cafeteria, I spotted Nash with his hand on the small of Alice's back as they waited for me. His fingers moved slowly, rubbing her in a tender way, and I thought that a girl couldn't help but love someone who treated her like that. Alice turned her head and smiled at him, and then she spotted me.

"Olivia, over here, hurry up!" she called out, waving frantically.

I joined them along the wall. "What?"

"Nash got his anniversary tattoo. Look."

Nash looked both proud and embarrassed as he rolled up his left sleeve. I held my breath, hoping that he hadn't put Alice's name forever in ink on his bicep.

He'd had a sword-wielding animated superhero character put there. It was a cross between a cat-like creature and a man, with claws and a tail. Flames surrounded the image. Nash looked thrilled. "Awesome, huh?"

"It's great, totally you," I agreed.

Alice squeezed his shoulders. "Nash loves body art. He wants to get another one for Christmas."

"What about you?" I asked Alice. "Any tattoos in your future?"

"Maybe a butterfly somewhere," she said. "But I don't know. I'm chicken about the pain."

"I won't lie to you, sweetie," Nash said. "It hurts."

We walked inside the cafeteria and went through the line. Hunger twisted my stomach. I stared at the food choices and smelled all the smells. I wanted to eat everything in sight. I selected the largest banana I could find. After finding a table and sitting down, I asked Alice if we were still going dress shopping on Saturday.

"Absolutely! We need to buy them before all the great ones in our sizes are gone. It's already late."

I began peeling my banana.

"What size are you now, anyway?" Alice asked. "Zero?"

"No!" I rolled my eyes. "Probably a four or a six."

"No way. You're smaller than that. I bet we can't find anything for you that won't need major alterations." She scowled at my banana.

I shrugged, pretending it was no big deal. "Then I'll get alterations. We have time."

Inside, though, I worried about having Alice see me trying on dresses. We'd seen each other naked, or nearly naked, lots of times—when we shared dressing rooms on other shopping trips or when we got ready for parties at her house or mine. On Saturday she would see a big difference in me.

How could I avoid that?

"We don't have a lot of time," Alice said.

True enough. I felt the press of time and the distance from my goal weight.

"Guess what?" I said, changing the subject. "Brody asked me out on another date tonight."

"Wow, things seem to be getting serious with you two," Alice said.

"I don't know about serious, but we're riding go-carts. I've advanced to 'Level 3' with him—whatever that means."

Alice chewed her lip a moment and then said, "I meant to tell you that I heard a few things about him not being such a nice guy."

"What kind of things?" I asked.

"He's really only after one thing, and once he gets it, he'll dump you."

I shook my head, not wanting to believe what she was saying. "That doesn't sound right. He and Erica dated for a long time."

"But he also cheated on her—more than once."

"Allegedly."

"Look," Alice said, "I'm just telling you what I heard. 'He's a creep. Don't trust him.' That's the advice from some of the girls who've gone out with him."

"I appreciate you looking out for me." But inside, I was thinking that Alice was the one who told me that jealous friends were the worst. And wouldn't anyone be jealous of the girl dating Brody Tipton?

Brody wasn't waiting for me at the vending machines. I went outside and looked around the parking lot, but he wasn't there either. For a few panicked minutes, I paced, thinking that maybe he'd stood me up and really *was* the jerk that Alice thought he was, but then his car drove up to the curb.

He rolled down the window. "Sorry, I'm late. Get in."

I opened the door and slid into the seat.

"No baseball practice tonight?" I asked.

"Something came up."

It sounded pretty clear that he didn't want to discuss whatever that something was.

"I've been looking forward to this all day," I tried again.

"Yeah, go-carts are pretty fun." He flashed me a smile. Then he reached down and turned on the radio, kind of loud. I didn't bother trying to talk over it. He seemed to be in a weird mood.

We drove to the Family Fun Center and bought tickets. The outdoor track had several loops and a ramp that circled and rose into the air to a tall slide-like structure. Drivers sped down the hill, braked, and made a sharp turn onto the winding track for another loop.

We waited in line for the current race to end. My heart pounded, and adrenaline coursed through my veins. What Brody didn't know was that I *loved* riding go-carts. Julian and I had come here all the time before he went away to school. He taught me how to drive aggressively, brake and accelerate, and even pick good cars.

I watched the drivers on the field carefully to see which go-carts were best candidates to jump into when the gate opened. Brody seemed distracted. He looked at the people in line and at nothing at all, but maybe he was a shark. Maybe he already had his car picked out.

Number twenty-three or number sixteen. Those were the possible ones I wanted when they pulled into the lineup. Number twenty-three had better positioning, but someone else snagged it first. Okay, number sixteen was mine. I could make up the time. Kids were easy to pass. They usually didn't know what they were doing on the track. Most adults didn't either.

As soon as the operator released us, I pressed the accelerator and pushed forward. Side-by-side, Brody and I broke through the line and onto the open track. I swerved to the outer side of the curve, passing as many people as possible before we approached the circular risers of the hill. Brody quickly realized that I knew what I was doing. He bumped me, sending my tail sideways, but I recovered and pushed ahead. We soon became the front runners and jockeyed for position.

I grinned at him. He grinned back. We raced up the hill. On the downward side, rather than braking, I pressed the accelerator and rushed past him, turning the wheel sharply before reaching the bottom of the hill and braking at the same time, the way Julian had taught me, so that my rear skidded and straightened the cart at just the right moment. I accelerated again and zoomed to the front of the pack. I picked up speed. I took a full car length ahead of Brody, and the engine in my cart was faster than his. I kept up the pace, taking the curves at just the right positions. I took the hill. Now, I was two lengths ahead as I hit the hill again, and I pulled the same maneuver, which gave me three lengths.

I easily won the first race. When we exited the lines, I grinned at Brody and said, "Good race. I didn't tell you before, but Julian taught me how to drive go-carts."

"I guess so," he said tightly.

"Do you want to go again?"

"No." He scowled at me.

"What do you want to do, then?" I asked, confused by his angry face.

"I'm hungry," he spat. "Let's go inside to the food court and get something to eat."

He strode toward the doors without waiting for my response. I wasn't sure if he was really hungry or just quitting because he was mad about losing.

I followed him inside. My stomach lurched. The food court was nothing but burgers, hot dogs, and fries. There was nothing on my diet that I could eat in here.

At the counter, Brody ordered a cheeseburger and fries with a large regular Coke. "What do you want?" he snapped at me.

I stared at the menu for a moment. "Just a Diet Coke."

"That's it?"

I could have lied to him and said I ate a protein bar at the gym before he picked me up, but I didn't feel like doing that.

"I'm still trying to lose a little weight for *prom pictures*," I said icily. "And nothing here fits with my diet plan."

We stared at one another. The girl behind the cash register shifted from one foot to the other. "Um, so will that be all?" she asked.

"Yes." Brody handed her some money.

I turned my back to him. I couldn't believe that he was mad at me for winning a race. Did he expect me to *let him* win? Was he one of those guys that couldn't stand to lose to a girl? Really?

Did I really want to date a guy like that?

"You should have told me that you and your brother came here and raced," he said. "I never would have let you pass me on that curve."

Let me pass? He didn't have an option. There was a clear opening, and I took it.

"I don't want to fight with you," I said.

"We're not fighting."

His food came up, and he went over to get the tray. He handed me a paper cup so that I could fill my own drink from the fountain machine. I thought of Nash and Alice. Nash always sent Alice to the table while he brought the drinks.

"Look, I'm sorry." He sighed. "I know I'm being a real butt about this, I'm sorry." He popped a fry into his mouth and gave me that dimpled grin. "Forgive me?"

Those blue eyes pleaded with me.

"We're both pretty competitive," I conceded. "I suppose it goes with the territory."

"You beat me on our first date, too."

"I still think you let me win on that one." I smiled.

"Maybe, maybe not."

I watched him finish eating. My stomach tied itself into a tiny knot of hunger, but it didn't make noises to betray itself, thank goodness. At last the torture was over.

He wiped the salt off his hands with a napkin. "So what now?"

"No more races or contests." I looked at my watch. "It's getting kind of late anyway, and I still have homework to do. Maybe we should just call it a night."

As we left the building, he casually took my hand and pulled me close to his side. This was what I wanted, to be together, to be holding his hand and feel like his girlfriend. We walked together in the open, for all the world to see, even if his grip seemed so loose that he might drop me at any moment.

We separated at the car. Inside, he turned on the radio again—this time to a heavy metal station that I didn't like—but I didn't say anything. His mood seemed dark again. He turned up the air conditioner, and I wrapped my arms around my body to ward off the chill. Each finger on each of my hands found a different rib, and I held them, fingers to ribs, counting, over and over.

What if Brody wasn't the right guy? What if I'd made a mistake?

I couldn't make a mistake.

116 / 110

April 4

Despite my best efforts, the scale on Saturday morning reported a huge disappointment. I looked so freaking fat in the mirror that I wanted to cry. How could I go dress shopping like this? I was as fat as a cow.

And to make matters worse, I knew I'd have to eat today because Alice would want to stop somewhere for lunch. It wouldn't be a good day; I couldn't stay on plan.

Since my afternoon shift started at four o'clock, Alice picked me up early so we could begin dress shopping as soon as the stores opened. We started with a popular bridal store. Half of the store shimmered in white and ivory satin, but the other half carried a diverse selection of colorful bridesmaid and prom dresses.

Alice's many bracelets rattled as she slid hangers along the rail and investigated the choices. She pulled one out and discovered that it had a mermaid-style skirt. "Yuck," she said. "These make me look too hippy."

I wrinkled my nose and nodded in agreement. Nothing caught my eye. Plastic rustled, and fabric whispered. I kept digging.

"What do you think of this one?" Alice asked.

I eyed the long, black gown in her hands skeptically. "I'm not sure. You should try it on and see," I suggested.

While she considered the dress, I took a royal blue one off the rack, shook my head, and put it back. Alice found something in pink that looked much more promising than the black one.

"Definitely," I said, "especially with your hair and skin tone."

"No luck?" she asked me.

"I want something… I don't know."

"You'll know it when you see it. We have lots of other stores to try. Don't give up hope. Let me try these on, though."

We went to the large dressing room area. Along one wall, there was a raised platform surrounded by mirrors where girls stood for the seamstress to take measurements for alterations. A bride in a white satin gown twirled there while her mother and friends gushed about the dress.

The fitting rooms were located down a narrow hallway. Alice motioned for me to follow her, but the spaces really weren't big enough for both of us to crowd inside together.

"I'll just be right here," I promised. "Open the curtain when you're ready."

She tried the first dress and didn't even show me. "You were right about the black," she called through the curtain. "Not for me."

"What about the pink?"

"Hold on..."

I waited, listening to the rustling of fabric. After a few minutes, she threw the curtain aside and twirled in front of me. "What do you think?" she asked.

I appraised the dress critically. "Too big."

"You think?"

"Yeah. It needs to be more fitted around your waist and chest. Let me see if there's a smaller size on the rack. Turn around." I looked at the size on the tag. "Okay, I'll be right back."

I returned to the floor and searched through the dresses, but I couldn't find the pink dress in the right size. I returned to her, shaking my head.

"You'll have to have it altered," I said.

She'd already changed into her clothes again.

"Let's go to the next place," she suggested. "We'll come back here if we don't find anything. That's only my first 'maybe.' I don't want to start talking about alterations until I've exhausted the city."

"We don't have all day," I reminded her. "I have to go to work."

"We can do this. Don't worry."

Next, we hit the mall. Several department stores carried prom dresses, especially the high-end store, and there was a boutique on the first floor. There, I found my dress. It was red, fitted, and floor-length, with a small train that flared off the back.

"I have to try this on!" I exclaimed. "Look!"

"That has potential," Alice agreed. "What size is it?"

"Six."

"I'm telling you that you're a two or a zero. Do they have one in that size?"

"I am *not* that small," I said, thinking of the scale that morning.

"Trust me. These dresses run big anyway. Just give it a try."

She followed me into the dressing room. It was huge, with plenty of room to spare, and she had two dresses of her own to try on. I couldn't send her away. Besides, she was already taking her clothes off. She slid her jeans down her legs, showing her round bottom and legs—not thin stilts, but not fat either. She had a poochy belly, which she was wiggling into the first gown. Curvaceous was the adjective to describe my best friend.

"You look lovely in that," I said.

"You think?" She twirled. It was a cream-colored chiffon A-line gown with a flowy skirt that made her look like a princess. The back plunged into a V.

"That style is so flattering on you," I said, and it was true. "It fits perfectly, no alterations. You have to get it."

"I don't know. It's a definite maybe. What about you? What are you waiting on?"

I looked at the red dress in my hands. Suddenly I wished I could ask her to turn her back and not watch me change, but I knew that would *not* go over well.

Putting the dress on a hook, I reached down and unfastened my jeans. I'd worn a loose pair, and they slid off my hips in one smooth motion. I kicked them aside and reached for the bottom of my sweater, pulling it over my head so that I stood in my bra and panties. There, she could see.

I tried to rip the dress off the hanger as quickly as possible, but those stupid little strappy things slowed me down.

"Oh, Olivia," Alice murmured from behind me.

I didn't say anything. I just kept fumbling with the hanger.

"What's happened to you?" Her voice was barely above a whisper.

Finally, the dress became freed. I pulled the zipper down and stepped through the opening, pulling the dress up and over my hips, sliding my arms through the holes.

"Zip me?" I asked, turning my back to her.

She didn't say anything for a second. I was afraid she wouldn't do it. Then I felt her hands at the base of my lower back, tugging at the fabric, and the zipper whistled up its track.

"Thanks," I said, twirling. "What do you think?"

She forced a smile, blinking tears. "It's lovely. It's the perfect dress."

It felt quite snug along my ribs, but I knew that after I lost those last six pounds, the dress would be comfortable, maybe even loose. I couldn't believe it was a size two. Was I really that tiny? They must make the sizes different at this store.

Alice reached out and touched my collarbone. "Sweetie, what's wrong? You can tell me."

I looked down. I could see the faint outline of ribs, my collarbone, and the knob of my shoulder. It all seemed so beautiful to me.

She looked at me with pity, not admiration.

I didn't understand. Tears welled up in my eyes.

"What? What is it?" she asked.

The words poured out of me. "I just wanted to slim down for the prom! I wanted to look gorgeous!"

"Oh, honey, you *do!* You look absolutely fabulous."

"Then why are you looking at me like I'm some kind of freak?" I began crying.

She bit her lip and tilted her lip to the side. Slowly, she walked around me. Returning to the front, she sighed. "I guess it's the shock. You've lost so much weight, so fast."

I sniffed. "And you think it's too much?"

She put her hands on my shoulders. "I think you're beautiful, Olivia. But no more, okay? No more."

Only six pounds more.

"No more," I agreed, wiping at the tears. "Maintenance only. I need to stay this size so I can still fit into the dress a month from now."

"I don't think you'll have any trouble with that."

I twirled away from her, avoiding her eyes and looking in the mirror instead. "Yes, this is definitely the dress. What about you?"

"I want to try this other one on first."

Alice changed dresses, but she went back to the chiffon A-line dress for her final choice. I agreed that it was the best one.

"Now, shoes," she announced.

Since my dress was so expensive, I searched for something on sale and found a pair of strappy red sandals with some silver bling that sort of matched the beading on the bodice of my gown. I skipped getting a purse or other accessories, but Alice went all-out.

We left the mall with time to spare.

HOLLOW BEAUTY

"Let's eat lunch somewhere," she suggested.

"Okay, but my treat. I appreciate you driving today—and helping me find my dress."

"Where do you want to go?"

I thought about my diet and the snug-fitting gown I'd bought. I was still six pounds away from my goal weight, and I'd just told my best friend that I wouldn't lose any more weight. Outright dieting in front of her would be harder from now on.

I named a restaurant where I knew I could get a low-calorie salad and stay in control. Blubber Busters gave great ideas for salads, like dipping the tines of your fork into the dressing to get a taste without a lot of calories.

We went to the restaurant and placed our orders. Alice pursed her lips when I bought the Diet Coke and light Italian dressing with my garden salad, but at least I was eating something. I hadn't planned on lunch at all.

"Maintenance," I reminded her. "And you have to admit that this is a lot more than a banana."

We picked up our meals and found a place to sit. She popped a regular fry into her mouth and leaned forward. "So tell me how things are *really* going with Brody," she said. "We don't get to talk girl talk with Nash around all the time."

I tried to decide how much to say. It was hard because I wasn't entirely sure how I felt. "I really like him. I mean, he's gorgeous, right?"

Alice nodded. "Totally. He's Brody Tipton."

I thought about our first date on the mini golf course. "And he can be so sweet…"

"I hear a 'but' coming." She sounded intrigued.

120

"I don't know. Sometimes I feel like something's off. I can't put my finger on it yet. It's like he's—on our last date, I beat him at go-carts. And he got all pouty and mad about it."

"Guys have huge egos."

"It was *go-carts*." I made a face, like duh!

"Testosterone."

I threw my hands in the air and shook my head. "Maybe you're right. Maybe that's all it is. It was just so weird. I thought he would be above that."

"It cripples the best of them, I'm afraid."

I thought about Ross. Testosterone or not, I didn't think he would have behaved the way Brody did at the end of the race. Ross would have congratulated me in a good-natured way, or maybe challenged me to a rematch, or both. He wouldn't have tried to sabotage my diet as payback.

I watched her eat several fries. At least they weren't curly fries; that would have been pure torture.

"So are you and Brody going out tomorrow?" Alice asked.

"No, I'm hanging out with Ross, my friend from the diner. Did I tell you about him?"

"No, who's that?" Her eyebrows shot up.

"He's taken me riding dirt bikes a couple of times on his grandfather's farm."

"Is he cute?"

I thought about Ross's hazel eyes, curly brown hair, and broad farm boy build. I thought about his scar and slight limp. I thought about his voice, deep and quiet and nice. "Yeah, but not in the way that Brody is. He's just a friend," I insisted. "We're just hanging out. It's no big deal."

"Does Brody know about him?"

"No."

"Does Ross know about Brody?"

"Yes. I wanted him to know up front that we were friends—nothing more."

She nodded and fiddled with her bracelets. "Okay, if you say so."

"I have a big brother. I'm capable of male friendships."

She smirked. "I'm not doubting you."

"Good." I could tell that she totally doubted me.

"It's just that you're being a little defensive about it, that's all," she said.

"Brody's the one I'm dating. Brody's the one I'm falling for, not Ross."

"And you're going to the prom with Brody, and you'll be wearing that fabulous dress, and you'll be beautiful."

Right.

115 / 110

April 5

On Sunday afternoon, as soon as we were in the truck and headed for his grandfather's farm, Ross wanted to know about my dress. "So what color did you get?"

I glanced over at him, shocked. "Really? You want to know about my prom dress?"

"It's important to you, so it's important to me." His deep voice actually sounded sincere about this.

"Red."

"What color of red? Rose red, blood red, maroon, magenta, fuchsia…"

I laughed. Magenta? Fuchsia? How many guys asked a question like that? "Blood red, I guess. It's *really* red, with some beading around the bodice where it's fitted, and it has a train."

"I bet you look like a bombshell in it." He looked away from the road and winked at me.

"I don't know about that." I blushed and quickly changed the subject. "How did you become interested in caving?"

He chuckled. "You don't take compliments very well."

"Right, so answer the question."

He rapped his hands on the steering wheel a few times. On the radio, an up-tempo country tune played softly, not intrusive. "Let's see," he began. "When I was twelve, my aunt and uncle came to visit us, along with some cousins, and my parents tried to think of some touristy things to do. Along with the Space and Rocket Center over in Huntsville and the aquarium in Chattanooga, we ended up going to Cathedral Caverns, and I was hooked. After that, I wanted to see every commercial cave in the area—DeSoto Caverns, Ruby Falls, Rickwood Caverns, Sequoyah Caverns, Russell Cave—I even visited Mammoth Cave in Kentucky."

"When did you start doing 'wild' caves?"

"My parents began to realize that I was getting more interested in caves, not less. I could recite all kinds of weird facts. Dad joined the grotto with me at first because he didn't want me doing it by myself, but once he saw that I was in good hands and I was fourteen, he let me go alone."

"Have you gone into any vertical caves?"

"No, but it's something I want to do. I don't have a lot of experience with the ropes, and as you can imagine, my parents aren't big fans."

"Your dad sounds really cool." I couldn't keep the jealousy from my voice.

"What's your dad like?"

"I don't know," I said. "He left when I was a baby."

"Oh, sorry."

"Don't be. From what Mom and Julian say, he was a jerk."

"Did your mom ever remarry?"

I shook my head. "She said she wasn't interested in going through that again. But I think she was scared to try dating again, especially with young children. It was easier to focus on working and raising us than to try to pursue another relationship."

"It must have been hard on her to be a single mom."

"My grandparents helped us a lot," I said.

"Are you close to them, then?"

"Nana, yes."

"What do you like most about her?" he asked.

"She smiles all the time. Her face is as wrinkled as a raisin, and her laugh is music to me. I feel happy whenever I'm with her, no matter how I was feeling before I went to her house."

He nodded. "She sounds nice."

"And she makes the best homemade blackberry jam. When they come into season, I'll pick them from the bushes in her backyard, and she'll make some for me. It's like heaven in your mouth."

"What about your grandfather?" he asked.

I turned my face toward the window. Pappy didn't like me very much. Julian never did wrong, but with me, Pappy always had some criticism.

"He's bristly," I said at last. "I honestly don't know how he and Nana go together."

Ross tapped his thumbs on the steering wheel some more. The turn for the dirt road was coming up soon.

"What makes you and your boyfriend go together?" he asked after a moment.

I took a sharp breath at the unexpected question. "Um, I don't know. We're both long-distance runners."

"So common interests bring you together?"

I thought about the bookstore and coffeehouse date where Brody droned on about baseball and how I thought he was kind of boring. He didn't like to read books, so we couldn't talk about those. I tried to think about Brody's voice when we talked on the cross country trails—or what we talked about—but I couldn't conjure the sound in my mind or the way it gave me shivers. Really, I couldn't think of many things that we had in common beyond running, but I didn't want to admit that. I didn't know how to explain what made us go together except to say that I wanted him. He was gorgeous and popular, and for some reason he'd chosen *me* for his prom date.

That sounded shallow; it had to be more than that.

"We've known each other for a couple of years," I said. "We've been friends, joking around on the team and just talking and stuff. I had a crush on him for awhile, but he didn't know. Then this spring, for some reason, he noticed me."

"How could he *not* notice you?" Ross gave me a sideways glance.

"For one thing," I said, "he only saw me in sweats and a ponytail. We didn't see each other in school when I looked halfway decent."

"I see you in a ponytail and a hideous Grace Lake Diner tee shirt with grease on your face, and I can tell how pretty you are."

"Ross…"

"I noticed you the first minute I walked out of the cooler. I'm just saying. Don't get a big head or anything." He turned onto the dirt road of his grandfather's farm. "I know you have a boyfriend. I'm glad you've chosen to spend some time with me this afternoon, and I'm grateful for the friendship and help."

"We're going to find your cave today," I said. "I can feel it."

In truth, I hoped we didn't find the cave right away because once we did, we wouldn't have an excuse to come out here, ride the dirt bike, and wander around in the woods together anymore.

That night, I felt too keyed up to fall asleep. Finally, I rolled out of bed and turned on my computer. I didn't feel like reading the Blubber Busters boards, though. I pulled up a search engine and looked up information on caving.

Alabama had lots of caves—over four thousand of them, according to one article I read. Most of them were "wild" caves like the one that Ross and I were searching for, but there were also a lot of State Parks and commercially-operated caves where tourists could walk through the cave with a guide. That might not be too bad. I couldn't imagine crawling through the muddy, wet tunnels of a wild cave.

I read about how caves formed in the limestone and learned about the difference between stalactites and stalagmites until I felt sleepy enough to return to bed. In my dream, I walked through a cave. Someone held my hand and went in front of me, wearing a helmet with a lamp attached to the front. He was a beacon of light in the darkness, my guide. His hand was warm and firm, holding tightly onto mine, not letting go. When he turned to check on me, I wasn't at all surprised that the face didn't belong to Brody, but to Ross.

What surprised me were my own feelings of relief and gladness.

114 / 110

April 7

The ceiling of my bedroom consisted of twelve-by-twelve inch tiles etched with random patterns. I couldn't make sense of them, just as I couldn't make sense of my second loss. Another track meet, another failure.

Here in my bedroom, lying on the soft carpet within the glow of the lamplight, I stared at the ceiling and counted all the bones my fingers could feel beneath my skin: ribs, hips, wrist, elbows, and collarbones. I measured the value of beauty and weighed it against the cost. Running had meant everything to me—until this spring, until the prom, until Brody.

I shifted my gaze to the purple walls surrounding me. Growing up, this room had been decorated in the theme of my favorite Disney characters from *Bambi*. Mom had stenciled them on the wall in a mural that remained until my sweet sixteen birthday, when we both agreed that I'd outgrown Disney. The stuffed animals, ceramic lamps, and other knick-knacks went to a charitable donation, and my pastel violet walls became a darker shade of purple, one more suitable for a teenager.

Running was the only thing that Pappy approved of, and probably only because Julian did it too. Pappy came to our 5K and 10K races and even took pictures of me at the finish line.

One time at a race, I took third place in my age group, and after receiving my medal in the award ceremony, he said, "Next time, maybe you'll get first place."

I tried harder. I ran longer distances, ran hill sprints, ran intervals until my lungs burned, and when I won that first place trophy, he smiled at me and ruffled my hair. "Good job," he said.

I stroked my stomach and the places on my body where I couldn't feel the bones, the places where fat still resided. Fat was the enemy. It made me ugly. Alice said I looked skinny now and didn't need to lose any more weight, but my clothes made me look thinner than I really was. People didn't see me naked like this. Naked and fat. Fat, fat, fat. Ugly. Even if I wanted to, I could never let a boy like Brody see me like this.

Or a boy like Ross.

Why did his name keep popping into my mind? He was just a friend. Brody was my boyfriend and the one I was dating. Brody was the guy taking me to the prom.

But when I ran my hands over the soft spots on my belly and closed my eyes, it was Ross's hands I imagined there.

I sat up and forced his face away from my thoughts. I unwrapped the towel from my damp hair and reached for the brush. Enough. I knew what I had to do. My goal weight was only four pounds away. I could do it.

I stood and put on my pajamas. On my night stand sat the letter. My first-choice college had rejected me. I'd sent several applications, including the big state schools, but I'd really wanted this one. Not getting in was a major blow, especially on top of my loss on the track. I was a double loser.

This thinking wasn't productive. I sat on the edge of my bed, picked up my phone, and sent a text to Alice.

Me: RU there?

I waited. No response. I went over to the computer and logged on to the Blubber Buster's boards.

Olivia: 5'4", 114 / 110: I'm feeling pretty low tonight. Anyone have help for the discouraged?

Molly: 5'0", 117 / 90: What's wrong, Olivia?

Olivia: 5'4", 114 / 110: I lost another track meet. Weak and dizzy. Plus, I didn't get into my first-choice college.

Molly: 5'0", 117 / 90: Sorry to hear about that (hugs). Didn't you have trouble with your track meet a few weeks ago?

Olivia: 5'4", 114 / 110: Yeah.

Molly: 5'0", 117 / 90: You need to eat some protein before you run—but not too much. You need some energy. You can't starve and race.

Olivia: 5'4", 114 / 110: But I'm so close to my goal.

Molly: 5'0", 117 / 90: Which is more important to you?

Olivia: 5'4", 114 / 110: ...Good question.

113.5 / 110

April 8

At lunch on Wednesday, Alice apologized for missing my text. "I had my phone turned off. Nash and I were at a movie."

"It's okay."

"What did you want?"

I stared at Alice's necklace for a moment. Today's ensemble consisted of a string of pale green stones on a thin silk necklace with matching, dangling earrings. A unique Alice creation. The color pulled out the green hue in her eyes.

"Nothing, really," I said. "Just to chat. I was feeling kinda bummed because of the meet yesterday."

She nodded, sending the earrings swinging. "I heard you didn't have a good run. I'm sorry."

I looked at my pathetically weak thighs.

"You want to talk about it now?"

I looked from her to Nash. "Not really."

"You want me to go?" Nash asked.

"No!" I said quickly. "It's okay. I'm fine. It's not you, Nash. I don't need to talk about anything."

Nash and Alice exchanged glances.

"You don't really seem fine, sweetie," Alice said.

To appease Alice, I'd bought a light, nonfat vanilla yogurt in addition to my banana. It slowed down my weight loss, but I needed to demonstrate my intention to stop dieting and go into maintenance.

I dipped my spoon into the yogurt and licked slowly, slowly. "I have a date with Brody tonight. We haven't gone out since the go-cart incident."

"Oh." Nash nodded.

I knew that Alice would have told him everything. There were no secrets among us.

"What do you guys think I should do?" I asked.

"Where are you going?" Alice asked.

"He never tells me ahead of time." I dipped my spoon again. It was hard to stop myself from gobbling the whole container in three huge bites, but I didn't. I licked. Slowly.

"You guys always seem to do something competitive—mini golf, go-carts... You've won each time, right?" Nash asked.

I hadn't thought about it that way, but I shot the hole in one on our first date and then raced to victory on go-carts. "Yeah."

"He needs a chance to save face. He's the big jock, Olivia. He's used to impressing people with his wins."

"Maybe you're right."

"I'm a guy," Nash said. "I know how we operate. Losing is a form of rejection."

I shook my head. On the trail, Brody never lost. His light frame and long legs gave him the perfect balance of speed and endurance to beat any competition. No one came close.

Could he really be so fragile that losing bruised his ego that much?

"Are you really saying that I should compromise my integrity and *let* him win?" The idea was ludicrous.

Nash shrugged. "What means more to you—winning some stupid game, or the guy?"

"But is the guy even worth it if he can't lose to a girl?" I asked.

Nash and Alice raised their eyebrows simultaneously.

"Rhetorical question, right?" Alice asked.

"Right."

"Just checking."

I finished my yogurt with one big spoonful of deliciousness. Then I pointed it at Nash, the representative male at the table. "Julian wouldn't get all upset like that if a girl he was dating beat him at go-carts."

"Your brother's smarter than Brody. He would never take a girlfriend to a place like that in the first place—at least not in the beginning of the relationship. Julian would stick to restaurants, movies, and holding hands."

I nodded. That's exactly what he would do.

"If Brody was smart," Nash continued, "he'd change tactics and do the same. Romance you. That's what I did with Alice."

He turned to give her a long kiss.

True love. Why couldn't I have that?

After track and baseball practice, Brody met me at the vending machines. "Where to tonight?" I asked.

"I don't know. What do you want to do?"

No competitive games. Nash's advice from lunch was still running through my mind. "How about a movie?" I suggested.

"Okay." He took my hand and walked with me to his car.

I couldn't tell whether or not he liked my suggestion. He stopped at a drive-up a fast food place where customers ordered burgers and shakes from their cars, and someone wearing roller skates brought the food out to the car. He turned off the engine.

Nothing on the menu was on my diet. Not one thing.

Suddenly, I couldn't take it anymore. I didn't want to sit beside Brody and starve while he enjoyed a thick burger and fries. I was too hungry. I was tired of being hungry.

Wasn't I thin enough? Almost thin enough? Wouldn't it be okay, just this once, to eat? It would set me back several days, but I'd make it up with extra running over the weekend.

Brody pushed the button and placed our order: two burgers and fries, one regular and one diet.

We sat in the seats, looking at each other, and then Brody reached across the console and clasped my hand. He squeezed.

"You look amazing now," he said. "You're getting so skinny."

"Thanks."

"You're almost as tiny as Erica Miller."

Almost. In the end, Erica Miller had been a willow of a girl, like a ballerina. Her arms and legs looked long and graceful, nearly translucent in their thinness.

His thumb rubbed back and forth on the back of my hand. He gazed into my eyes. The blue of his irises was hypnotic. I stared into them, caught, and after a moment, he leaned toward me. His hand released mine and rose to the back of my neck, pulling me in for the kiss. My lips softened and allowed full access to everything.

His hands splayed into my hair, and the kiss deepened. I tried to enjoy it. Brody Tipton was kissing me! But instead, my mind wandered over how weird his breathing was and how the console was digging into my side, and nothing felt very romantic in this at all.

A knock came at the window. Brody broke away, smiling. "I guess that's our dinner."

I nodded, and when he turned to reach for it, I wiped my lips with the back of my hand.

He turned back with the sodas, and I put them into the cup holders in the center console. Then he handed the food to me and paid the girl. I unwrapped the sandwiches. They smelled heavenly. I hadn't eaten a burger in more than a month. My mouth watered in anticipation. I ate a French fry.

"Mmm," I said.

"How can you eat like that and still lose weight?" he asked.

I shrugged and pretended. "I've been running a lot. Besides, one hamburger isn't going to make me fat." To prove my point, I took a huge bite of the sandwich and chewed. It tasted wonderful. I wanted to gobble the whole thing, but he was watching me.

"I know that," he said.

I decided to eat only half of the burger in front of him and maybe a handful of fries. To help curb my appetite, I took a big gulp of Diet Coke. Then another.

Brody worked on his hamburger without a care, but I counted each bite and every French fry. After I'd eaten what seemed like too much, I wrapped the remainder of my sandwich back up and declared, "I'm stuffed."

"Really?"

"My stomach's shrunk from my diet. You want the rest of my fries?"

"Sure!"

I drank my soda and watched him eat. I thought about Ross and realized that if he and I were sitting here together, we'd be blathering on and on about all kinds of things. Why was Ross so easy to talk to, but Brody wasn't? Hadn't we talked more on the cross country trail? I thought so, but I couldn't remember what we talked about anymore.

"What movie do you want to see?" I asked.

He shrugged. "I don't know what's playing."

I named a few titles.

"Never heard of them," he said.

I gave a plot summary of some.

He grunted.

I gave up and leaned back in the seat. Brody went to throw away our garbage, and then we headed to the theatre.

After a few moments of consideration, we decided to watch a romantic comedy. We were early, but we went in and found good seats. As the pre-movie commercials played, Brody leaned over and began kissing me again in the semi-darkness. I tried harder to concentrate and respond to his lips, and when he slipped his fingers beneath the hem of my shirt, I didn't jerk away.

Let him win, Nash had said.

Tonight's game was making out at the movie theatre, and since there was only so far he could go here, I felt safe.

His breath felt hot against my mouth, and then his lips traveled against my throat, pressing and kissing, and his fingers danced lightly against my stomach as if deciding whether to head north or south. He made a sound in his throat and pulled me closer, so that the arm rest jammed against my hip.

His fingers traveled north and traced the outline of my bra. I thought about what he was doing. No boy had ever touched me like this before, and I felt oddly disconnected from the whole thing. Brody's kisses didn't ignite any fires in me. I wanted them to. When I looked at him, my stomach did that funny little thing, but the actual kiss was a disappointment. It was hard to explain. Like coffee, which smelled so rich and wonderful brewing in the pot, but I couldn't stand its bitter taste.

Meanwhile, Brody's fingers found the clasp of my bra and began working the hook. That was the line.

"No, not here," I whispered, pulling away.

He gave me a pouty look but didn't seem entirely surprised. If anything, he couldn't believe he'd progressed as far as he had.

The lights went down, and the movie began. He leaned over and whispered in my ear. "When?"

I gave him a panicked look. When what?

"How about the prom?" He gave me a half smile. "Although I don't know if I can wait that long—can you?"

I opened my mouth, frozen, unable to say yes or no.

He took my hand and squeezed before leaning over and whispering, "It's okay, you don't have to be afraid. I know how to be gentle."

He settled into his chair, as if I'd said yes, as if the prom was a done deal from his perspective. Was this what it meant to let him win? Was I willing to go that far?

Eating that burger with Brody opened some kind of flood gate with me. That night after Mom went to bed, I crept downstairs and went into the kitchen. Everything was dark and silent except my heart hammering in my chest. My stomach was full, not hungry, but still I opened the pantry doors and pulled down a box of snack crackers and spray cheese. I ate until the cheese stopped spraying. I polished off an already open bag of chips. Then I switched to sweets. There was a box of frosted sugar cookies on the counter, and I devoured nine or ten of those.

Tomorrow I would return to plan. Tomorrow I would be good again.

So tonight, I had to eat everything. I had to swallow as much as I could hold so that it would be enough to carry me through the next month. Feast before the famine.

My belly ached. I felt bloated and sick. I stopped only because I had no more room to fill, and I went back upstairs to bed. But I couldn't sleep. I lay there, hating myself for my weakness, calling myself a loser, feeling physically ill, wishing I could take back what I had done. Already, I could feel the fat cells swelling beneath my skin and plumping me up again.

113 / 110

April 12

Four days later, my weight had at least returned to where it was on the day when I'd binged. I was frustrated with myself for messing up like that, but I needed to look forward, not back.

Only three pounds away from my goal.

At Grace Lake Diner, the Sunday breakfast rush dragged. All I could think about was riding with Ross that afternoon. When he arrived shortly before the end of my shift, my heart did somersaults. There was something arresting about the way he looked as he sat at the end of the counter in his long-sleeved checkered shirt, wild brown curls at the nape of his neck, hazel eyes watching me steadily while he sipped his drink and waited.

"You and Ross are getting pretty cozy, aren't you?" Sally asked in the kitchen when she realized that he had come for me and that I was rushing to finish and leave.

"No! Why?"

"Nothing." She put her hands in the air in an act of surrender. "I'm just saying, you two seem to be spending a lot of free time together."

"We're friends, that's all."

She stood at the steam table and stirred one of the dishes. "What are your plans for today?"

"Riding dirt bikes."

"Sounds fun."

"It is." I pulled the rack of clean dishes out of the machine and began stacking platters on the overhead shelf.

"He's a cute kid," she observed. Fishing.

I put the empty rack under the counter. "Okay, that's it for me. See you Friday night."

She smirked. "Have a good time today, Olivia. Don't do anything I wouldn't do."

"We're *friends*," I insisted.

"Uh-huh." She turned her back and went to flip some burgers on the grill.

I grabbed my bag of clothes and headed to the restrooms to change. Sally's teasing bothered me because it rang true. Ross *was* a cute kid, and we *were* getting cozy. I felt guilty about that. Maybe I liked him too much.

Once in my riding clothes, I walked over to Ross and leaned against the counter.

"You ready?" he asked.

"Please, let's get out of here before Sally gives me something else to do."

"Aren't you going to be too hot wearing that?"

I was wearing an oversized sweatshirt. "This is my riding shirt. I can get it filthy, and besides, it's chilly when we're going fast."

"It's pretty nice out there today."

"I'm fine, let's go." The truth was that I was always cold, all the time. It could be a hundred degrees out there.

"You want to grab something to eat first?" he asked.

"No thanks, I'm all set."

"Okay, let's go then." He slid off the stool.

I tossed my stuff in the trunk of my car and then walked over to the truck. Ross waited for me beside the passenger door and opened it for me.

"Watch your step. Those running boards are slippery," he said.

After I settled into the seat, he closed the door and joined me in the cab. He fired up the diesel engine, and we headed down the road. I studied his hands on the steering wheel. He didn't wear any rings, just the ordinary bumps, burns, and scars from fingers accustomed to laboring in dangerous places, like Sally's kitchen.

"You've lost a lot of weight since I met you," he observed.

My eyes shot in his direction, wondering what had prompted his comment. "A little."

"A lot," he insisted. "At least fifteen pounds, I'd guess."

I continued staring at him. "How can you tell that from looking at me?" I thought my sweatshirt covered everything.

"Why are you losing weight?" His deep voice sounded kind, even worried.

"How can you tell that I have?"

"I notice everything about you."

There he went again, making me blush. "Ross…"

"It's everything," he said. "How your jeans fit now. The size of your wrist when your shirt slides back as you reach for the handle to pull yourself into the truck. It's the shadows beneath your eyes and the prominence of your cheekbones. You've lost a lot of weight. Why?"

I sighed. I thought about my last date with Brody and how conflicted he'd made me feel. He'd wanted me to lose weight and praised my progress, and then he sabotaged me by taking me out for fast food. The binge might have been my own choice, but he'd made it difficult for me.

"It's a competition," I said.

"For what?"

"To see if I can get skinnier than this other girl from my school."

He frowned at me. "Why would you do that?"

"It's not dumb."

"I didn't say it was." He cut his eyes sideways at me.

"Your tone did."

"Okay, it's dumb," he admitted. "Why would you do that?"

"Because I like challenges. I want to see if I can do it."

"Who is this girl?" he asked. "Why does her weight even matter to you?"

I chewed on my lip. If I said it out loud, it would really sound dumb. But it wasn't—not to me.

"Olivia?"

I folded my arms across my chest. "She's a girl that Brody used to date."

"Oh, I see."

"No, you don't see anything!" I said.

"You're insecure and jealous of his ex."

"What? No! That's not it at all!"

"Yes, it is." Ross sounded very confident.

"For your information, *Brody* challenged *me*. When he asked me to the prom, he suggested that I could lose some weight, and I agreed with him."

Ross took his eyes away from the road to stare at me.

I waved him back to the windshield. "You're making me nervous."

He pulled over on the side of the road and put the truck into park. "You are *not* fat, Olivia!"

"Not fat, but I was *fluffy*. I was!"

"No, you weren't." His voice became stern. "What's wrong with this guy? Why are you even listening to him?"

"I knew you wouldn't understand. I never should have told you."

"No, tell me." He put his hand on my shoulder, but I shrugged him away. "Olivia?"

I stared out the passenger window with a huge burning lump in my throat.

"You're beautiful," he said, lowering his voice.

I shook my head.

"How can I make you believe me?" he murmured.

"It's nice to hear you say that, but—"

"Then I'll keep saying it until you believe it. You're beautiful."

That lump in my throat kept growing. I covered my face with both hands. "Are we going to find a cave today, or are we just going to sit here beside the road and flap our jaws?" My voice trembled. Tears threatened to fall.

"Definitely caving," he said. He threw the gearshift into drive and signaled to pull onto the road again.

I leaned my head against the headrest and closed my eyes, trying to pull myself together. For a moment, I allowed myself to fantasize that Ross reached across the console and took my hand. That helped. I imagined that his palm was warm and dry. His kisses didn't make me want to pull away; they made me want to push forward for more.

I wished he was the one taking me to the prom instead of Brody.

112 / 110

April 14

On Tuesday morning, I decided to win the 1600m and 3200m events at the track meet. I didn't run hill sprints before school. Instead, I followed the advice from my friends on the Blubber Busters boards to load up on protein. I ate two hard-boiled eggs for breakfast.

It felt scary to break my routine. Just two weeks stood between me and prom night, and I still had two pounds to go. Things had been moving too slowly.

I could make it, though. I could win this track meet *and* be skinnier than Erica Miller.

At lunch, I bought the grilled chicken sandwich and removed the bun, eating only the chicken, a yogurt, and two bananas. Alice looked at my tray with surprise and pleasure.

Slowly, I licked the vanilla yogurt from my spoon and watched Alice gobble the French fries and chicken sandwich with mayonnaise. Her chin moved up and down as she chewed, and her earrings dangled back and forth. She said something to me.

"What?" I asked. "I'm sorry, I wasn't listening."

"You're in another world over there."

"What did you say?"

"Nash and I were wondering if you and Brody would eat dinner with us on prom night. We could all go together somewhere. It would be fun."

"I'll ask him. We're going out Thursday."

"We were thinking maybe that new place out by the mall that just opened. Have you been there yet?"

"No."

"I'm getting excited, aren't you? It's only two weeks away!"

"I know, I can't wait." But I was worried now that Brody thought we might do something more than dance at the prom. I still didn't even know how to think about that.

Alice and I had talked about sex before, especially when she and Nash first crossed that line in their relationship—which had been a long time ago. Losing her virginity had been a big deal and something wonderful for them. They were "in love." I wasn't so sure that losing my virginity to Brody would be nearly as special. I didn't think I felt things with him in the same way that Alice and Nash felt for one another. Brody's kisses didn't exactly set me on fire; sometimes he even grossed me out.

I'd always planned on waiting, not necessarily until marriage, but at least until sometime in college. High school seemed too soon. For one thing, I'd never had a serious enough boyfriend, and I wasn't even sure that Brody counted as that.

On the other hand, I *was* curious. I knew the reality of sex was probably a lot of nose-bumping awkwardness, but I couldn't help wishing for the fantasy of *Shakespeare in Love* or something like that, of being unwrapped like a precious gift and handled as tenderly as can be. My skin yearned for that kind of love.

At the track meet that afternoon, Coach Wilby approached me while I was stretching my calves.

"How are you feeling this afternoon, Olivia?" he asked.

"Good."

He nodded. He looked like he wanted to say more but was afraid to upset me before the race. I was grateful for his hesitation. I didn't need one more person expressing concern about my weight or diet or anything else.

"Great, actually," I said to further reassure him. "I feel really confident about the 3200 today."

"What about the 1600?"

"They have a pretty good miler, don't they?" I asked. "They did last year."

"*You're* a pretty good miler."

I made a face. "It's not my best event. You know that."

"Just do your best." He patted my back. "I know you will."

I looked across the field. Tammy had finished the pole vault and was heading my way. I continued stretching and waited for her to join me.

"How'd you do?" I asked.

She smiled. "First place!"

I gave her a high five. "Excellent, congratulations."

"Was Coach Wilby over here giving you a pep talk?" she asked.

"Yeah."

"How are you feeling?"

"Not you too!"

"Sorry, everyone's worried about you, that's all."

"I'm doing great today, thanks."

"Good, because I'm tired of kicking your butt out there. I can't carry this whole team myself." She grinned and bumped my shoulder with hers.

"Okay, I'll get out there and do my part."

"Glad to hear it." She crossed her arms, and we watched the next event set up. "I hear you and Brody are becoming quite the item."

"What does that mean?"

"A friend of mine saw him kissing you at your locker the other morning."

I shrugged. "Yeah, so?"

"Public displays of affection. Serious relationship."

"We've gone on a couple of dates. I don't know if that qualifies as a 'serious relationship.'"

"Just be careful with him," Tammy said. Her dark eyes looked concerned.

"I know, I will."

"He's a big flirt."

"You think I don't know that?"

"I'm just saying that he might not be as exclusive as you," she said.

"Why, do you know something? Is he seeing someone else?"

"No, it's not that."

"Then what?" I asked.

"I don't want to see you get hurt. That's all."

I looked across the track. It was almost time for the 3200m. "Well, like I said, we've only gone on a couple of dates. We're going to the prom. It's not like either of us ever said it was anything else."

I thought about Ross, who knew about Brody. Brody didn't know about my friendship with Ross, though, and I hadn't told him because I didn't think he'd understand. In truth, I felt as guilty about being non-exclusive as Tammy was implying that Brody was—at least in my heart. Just the other day, hadn't I wished that Ross was the one taking me to the prom instead?

It was time for our event. Tammy and I went to the starting line. Our competition checked us out. I leaned forward slightly, relaxed, and waited for the pistol.

At the sound, I sprinted for the first curve. Tammy and I raced with their front runner for the first lap, and then the three of us settled into a fast pace for the remainder of the laps. The girl had endurance. I pushed. Running, my whole body hurt. Each step jarred my bones painfully. My muscles were disappearing, and all that was left was skin stretched over bone and cartilage. Slam, slam, slamming against the pavement.

However, all that protein did its magic, and I had more energy this time than in races over the last few weeks. With two laps to go, I dug deeper and found another gear. Tammy and the other girl fell behind. I pushed to the final lap and the finish line with at least five seconds to spare.

Tammy crossed in second place.

I straightened up and looked out over the track. Protein, eh? Who knew? All I needed was some fuel to find my groove again.

After showering, I was heading toward the doors and the parking lot when I ran into Coach Wilby near the vending machines.

"Do you have a minute to talk?" he asked.

"Um…" I didn't want to talk to him. I was afraid of what he might say.

"It'll just take a minute." He took a step closer to me. "Great job today. Excellent. *That* was the Olivia I remember."

"Thanks."

He stared at me intently with his froggy eyes. I swallowed.

"Is everything okay, Olivia?" he asked, finally.

"Everything's fine."

He cleared his throat. "I can't help but notice how much weight you've lost recently—and how your performance on the track has suffered this spring."

I straightened my back. "I ran just fine this afternoon."

He nodded. "You were great. But you've really been struggling lately, in practice as well as during meets." He stared at me, and I was afraid that he was going to say something really negative about dieting. But his eyes filled with compassion. "I'm very concerned about you. I want to help."

A burning lump formed in my throat. "I don't need any help."

"I think you do," he said quietly.

I felt cornered, like if I didn't say something, he was going to keep hounding me about this. An idea suddenly came to me. "I've been sick," I blurted out.

"What kind of sick?"

"Food poisoning," I lied. "It was really bad. I'm going to be okay and everything, but that's why I've lost some weight. It's taken awhile for my appetite to come back."

His expression softened. "Oh, Olivia. I'm sorry. I had no idea." He nodded his head. "I ate a rotten hamburger once and vomited all night long. And of course, there was intestinal distress, too. I was sick for days. That's serious business."

I lowered my head, feeling ashamed for lying, but relieved as well because I knew he'd stop asking questions now. "I appreciate that you care about me, Coach Wilby. I really do."

He put his hand on my shoulder. "You've been running on this team since middle school. I've watched you grow up. How could I not care about you?"

Tears began gathering in my eyes. "Thank you," I murmured.

"Are you sure you should be running? Maybe you should take the rest of this season off."

"No way! It's my senior year. I'm not quitting!"

"We're talking about your health here. What do your doctors say?"

"That it's fine. I wouldn't be here if they didn't approve. Mom wouldn't let me."

We stared at one another. After a moment, he sighed and removed his hand. "All right. I'm glad you told me what's going on."

"Yeah." I hitched my bag higher on my shoulder and turned to leave.

"And Olivia?"

Why wouldn't he just let me go? "Yes?"

"Promise me that you'll take better care of yourself and get well."

I nodded. "I will."

112 / 110

April 16

On Thursday night after practice, Brody and I went out again. He took me to a minor league baseball game. It was already in progress when we arrived, but the score was still zero-zero. We hadn't missed much.

"You want a hot dog or something?" he asked, stopping in front of the concession stand.

I was so close to my goal weight. Today was a good day. I couldn't give in. Shaking my head, I said, "No thanks, just a Diet Coke, if that's okay."

"Sure." He placed an order for two dogs for himself and the drinks. Then we went to the bleachers and found seats. It wasn't very crowded.

I sat beside him and looked at the field. Brody took a bite of his hot dog and grinned. "Isn't this great?"

"I think you love baseball more than cross country."

"Heck yeah. I'd love to get picked up by one of the scouts and play minor league. I don't have any illusions about playing for the majors, but this... maybe."

"You're going to college, aren't you?"

"I've applied to a few places. I hope to get a baseball scholarship."

"I just received an acceptance letter yesterday," I offered.

"Oh yeah?" He continued eating his hot dog and watching the game.

"Samford University, in Birmingham. It's a great school. Even though it wasn't my first choice, I'm really excited."

"Cool."

I looked at him. I wondered if he'd actually heard me. I wondered if he cared about what I wanted to study.

"I'm thinking about majoring in basket weaving."

He nodded. "That's great."

I narrowed my eyes. "With a concentration in nothing."

He slurped his drink. With his other hand, he reached over and took mine. I pulled away.

"You're not even listening to me," I said.

"I'm watching the game. That's why we're here."

"Oh, I thought we were on a date. To, you know, get to know each other before the prom."

He looked at me for a moment. "You hate baseball, don't you?"

"I don't *hate* baseball."

"I don't want to make you do anything you don't enjoy. We can find something else."

"This is fine. I just—I want us to talk more."

He threw his arm around my shoulders. "Baseball is a numbers game. You see this guy over here?" He pointed to one of the players and began explaining the strategy of the current play. I tried to pay attention. I tried to get into his world and enjoy the evening.

We sat there for a couple of hours, and finally, I couldn't take it anymore.

"Brody, I know the game's not over yet, but it's late and a school night, and baseball's not over until it's over. We could be here until midnight."

"You want to go home?"

"Yes."

He sighed. "You're right."

We stood and made our way down the bleachers and out to the parking lot, holding hands. With my other hand, I stifled a yawn. Mom would be surprised to see me come home this late; we would push right against my curfew.

We didn't talk much on the drive to my house, and I closed my eyes, dozing. It didn't take long before Brody pulled into my driveway. He shut off the engine and lights. I opened my eyes.

He leaned across the console and kissed me before I even knew what was coming. For the first ten seconds, that kiss was everything dreamy that kisses were meant to be. His lips felt soft and warm, questioning. His hands stayed in my hair.

I wrapped my arms around his neck in response. His hand moved lower and grazed the side of my breast. I inhaled, and his lips pressed harder against mine, teeth grinding, tongue probing. The dreaminess became something else, and instead of wanting him to continue, I wanted to escape.

Pulling away, I forced a smile. "Thanks for tonight. I had fun."

"No, you didn't," he said. "But we *could* have some fun…"

"Brody."

"We've waited a long time for this."

We had? "We just started dating."

"You didn't feel anything for me last fall?" He nuzzled my neck for a moment.

"Yes, but—"

"Stop thinking about it so much, then. Give in to your feelings."

"Brody." I looked at my house and put my hand on the door. "I have to go inside. It's past my curfew."

"There's no curfew on prom night," he said. "You're mine from dance till dawn. What about then?"

He gazed at me with intense blue eyes. I didn't know what to say. I felt trapped.

"I'll think about it," I stammered. I opened the door, and the light glared on both of us.

He scowled. "I can't wait around forever, you know."

"I'll see you tomorrow." I shut the door and hurried toward the house without looking back. The lights flashed across the house as he backed up. Tires chirped as he drove away.

Mom had left a kitchen light on for me, but she didn't wait up. I went to the bathroom to brush my teeth and take off my makeup. I looked at my face in the mirror. Was I crazy for putting Brody off? Was I crazy for even considering sex with him?

I thought about the way his kiss had felt in the beginning, before I'd come fully awake. The softness. Maybe the problem was me. I couldn't relax. When I was half asleep, I was able to experience Brody's kisses as the wonderful, romantic things that they really were. Then I tensed up.

Maybe if I drank alcohol, I wouldn't get so scared and unable to enjoy intimacy with someone that I'd liked for a long time. Not a lot, just half a wine cooler or something.

If I suggested this, I was sure that Brody could arrange to have alcohol for the after-prom party.

111.5 / 110

April 19

On Sunday, Ross and I rode the dirt bike into the woods of his grandfather's farm again in search of the cave. We'd covered quite a bit of land in the past three weeks without any sign of it. Sometimes I doubted its existence at all; maybe the cave was just Ross's excuse to get me out here with him and—what? No, he hadn't made any big moves on me. We simply talked our heads off.

I took off my helmet and followed Ross into the woods of our latest search site. Most trees had fully opened their leaves, and various ones were flowering. Temperatures were warm today, but not too hot or humid.

Ross, the one who'd had a smashed pelvis, walked better than I did on the rugged terrain; I tripped over every vine and rock in my path.

"Sally's going to let me cook Thursday night," he said as we hiked up the hill.

"On your own, really?"

"She says I'm ready. My apprenticeship is complete."

"You'll have to cook me something," I said without thinking.

He lowered his voice. "I would love to feed you, Olivia. Anything you want."

The sexy way he said it sent a pulse through my insides. I cleared my throat and scrambled to change the subject to a lighter topic. "As long as it's on the menu, right?"

"Right. No crème brulee—at least not yet."

"Well, you'd better not mess up Thursday night. Sally will never let you behind the grill again if you do."

"Oh, ye of little faith. I'm not going to mess up."

"You're brave. I'm still thinking about asking Mr. Lee if I could train to waitress this summer and take some shifts."

He stopped to hold a branch for me. "Why don't you?"

I shrugged. "It terrifies me," I confessed. "Dishwashing is easy, comfortable, not *public*."

"Be courageous. Ask. You can do it."

"It's one of those things. Once I ask, then I'm committed to go forward." I began walking again, passing him. I didn't want to talk about this.

He joined me. "You want the extra money, right?"

"I *need* the extra money for books and college fees. I forgot to tell you. I received my acceptance letter to Samford University."

"That's great news, Olivia! Congratulations! Awesome! Is that where you want to go?"

"Yeah, I think so. It's a great school." I nodded.

I stumbled over another stupid vine. Ross caught my elbow, and we kept walking. My arm seemed to burn where he'd held me. What was wrong with me this afternoon?

160

"What do you want to study?" he asked, seemingly unaffected by my presence.

I needed to get a grip.

"Pre-law."

"Really? Wow." He looked at me and chuckled with that deep voice of his. "You want to be a lawyer, but you're afraid to try waitressing. That seems like such a contradiction. How are you ever going to manage closing arguments?"

"Well, maybe I won't do courtroom law."

"Why limit yourself? Come on, practice with me. Pretend I'm a customer at the diner."

"You're not a customer."

"I'll be disgruntled. Grr. Bring me a cup of coffee, wench."

I laughed. "Coming right up, sir. Would you like to order breakfast this morning?"

"Two eggs, over medium, and make sure the whites are cooked. You hear me? No runny whites. And bacon, well done, but not black. And white toast with apple butter."

"Got it."

"Repeat it back to me."

"Um… two eggs, bacon, toast, apple butter," I stammered.

"You'd better get all those special instructions to the cook—me—or you might end up with runny whites, and Mr. Disgruntled Customer is going to yell at you."

Grateful for the advice, I asked, "Is there some shorthand or something that I need to learn?"

"Most of the waitresses abbreviate things, but I can figure it out."

We went over the crest of a hill and entered a small clearing in the middle of the forest. Wildflowers grew in the grassy area among the boulders that lay everywhere, like forgotten toys of giants.

I stopped suddenly. "Hey, what is this place?"

"It looks like a good place to rest," Ross said.

He climbed on one of the flat boulders and stretched out in the sun. I found a spot beside him, close but not touching. The sky above us was blue and cloudless.

"What's your brother like?" I asked him.

"He's two years older than me. Married—"

"Married?"

"Yeah, he didn't want to do the college thing. He wanted to work the farm, raise a family… we're different in that way. He's more like Dad. I'm a bookworm like Mom."

"Julian and I are both bookworms," I said. "He's in graduate school, so I don't see him very much. I miss him."

"Are you close?"

"We were, growing up, even though we're six years apart. Julian always looked out for me."

"Big brothers are supposed to look out for little sisters."

"Yeah, I guess so." I squinted at the sky. "Are you and your brother close?"

"The way brothers are. We grew up playing together, fighting, watching out for each other, and all of that. At the same time, like I said, we have very different personalities and interests. He'd never read a novel. Spring planting never appealed to me."

"You didn't like driving the tractor?" I asked.

"Not really."

"But you like dirt bikes."

He chuckled. To my ears, it was a low, purring sound. "They're pretty different, you know. Two wheels versus four. Speed. Purpose…"

I swallowed. I knew he was looking at me, but I kept my eyes on the sky, where it was safe. "I like riding the dirt bike, too. I'd never been on one until I met you."

"I'm glad you like it," he murmured.

I pulled my legs up, so my feet sat flat on the rock and my knees pointed upward, and pressed my lower back into the rock. This felt so good and right, just lying here in the sun and talking to Ross.

I wondered what it would feel like if he rolled over and kissed me. Would I feel that panicked need to escape that I always felt when Brody kissed me? When I thought about kissing Ross, I felt nothing but excitement. Warmth spread through my body. It seemed impossible that he couldn't sense the electricity of my thoughts. If I turned my head right now and looked at him, just one look, he'd know. Our eyes would meet, and he'd immediately see that I wanted to kiss him more than anything, right here in the woods. All I had to do was turn my head.

The silence stretched out.

Be courageous, he'd said. Act.

The butterflies went wild in my stomach. I felt so much yearning inside of me. Desire. But I couldn't do it. Instead I swung my legs over the side of the rock and sat up. "We should go," I said, turning my back to him. "That cave's waiting for us."

110 / 110

April 21

On Tuesday morning, like every other morning, I went to the bathroom first thing and peed every extra bit of fluid possible. I stripped my pajamas off, then turned on the light. The scale was one of those electronic ones that was supposed to be super accurate. I pushed the button with my toe and waited for the digital readout to display zeros.

The scale had become my ultimate judge, critic, and friend. It told me the truth whether I wanted to know it or not. It determined whether I was good or bad, beautiful or ugly, thin or fat, successful or a failure, winner or loser. It determined my value. With one number, in one instant, the scale set the tone for my entire day.

I stepped onto the pad and waited.

The scale measured my efforts of the past twenty-four hours: every lap around the track, every hill stride, every morsel of food that passed between my lips, every ounce of fluid.

I waited.

Each morning was the same as this. Each morning I stood on the scale with a combination of dread, anxiety, hope, and anticipation. Before Brody, I never weighed myself. As long as my clothes fit, who cared? Now, the number on the readout between my feet had become more important than the number on Coach Wilby's stopwatch.

110.0.

I'd finally reached my goal weight!

I'd crossed the finish line.

I'd won.

I stepped off the scale and looked at myself in the mirror, trying to see how much better I was at one hundred and ten pounds than I'd been at one hundred and twenty-nine. I turned sideways and sucked in my stomach, then let it hang naturally. I poked a bit of fat that clung stubbornly at my side. Just a little, but I could see it.

Erica Miller had lost something like twenty pounds for the prom. Wasn't that what Brody said?

She'd beat me by one pound. To win, I really needed to lose thirty.

This bit of fat at my waist would disappear if I dropped to one hundred. Besides, Jane and I were the same height, but her goal weight was one hundred. That must be the perfect weight for our height, rather than one hundred and ten. Obviously, I still had room for improvement. Look at that ugly fat.

I needed to be thinner. I bet I could do it.

109 / 100

April 23

On Thursday after track practice and a quick shower, I headed for the vending machines to meet Brody for our date. He was leaning against the wall wearing jeans and a white button-down shirt. His honey blonde bangs fell over his blue eyes, and he raked them sideways with his hand. He gave me a dimpled smile and pushed away from the wall. I caught a whiff of cologne.

"What do you have planned for tonight?" I asked.

"No more baseball, I promise." He took my hand, and we walked toward the doors. "It's a surprise, but you're going to like it."

We passed a group of girls from the track team on our way to his car. They were standing in the parking lot, talking, and they saw me walking with Brody Tipton and holding his hand. Brody was the kind of guy I'd always dreamed of falling in love with. He was a confident, good-looking senior, well-liked and popular; he was a star athlete on the high school baseball team. His face had those chiseled cheekbones. Any one of those girls would love to be dating him and going to the prom with him. I felt lucky.

We got into the car, and Brody pulled out of the parking lot. I wondered where we were going and hoped it was going to be someplace fun.

"Can you believe the prom is next Saturday?" I asked to fill the silence.

"I guess you have your dress and everything."

"I told you. It's red, remember?"

"Oh, yeah. Right." He reached over and turned up the air conditioning. "You're going to look so hot."

"What do you want to do for dinner that night? Alice asked if we'd like to share a table with her and Nash at—"

"I've made reservations already. We're going with a group from the team and their dates."

"Oh." I leaned forward and turned the cold vents away from me.

He looked over at me. "I'm sorry I didn't ask you ahead of time. I just thought that it would be okay."

"It is. I mean, we never talked about anything. I guess we shouldn't have waited until the week before the prom to talk about the prom."

"We've been too busy having fun."

"Right." I smiled. "You've made me really curious about what we're going to do tonight."

He gave me a mischievous smile in return. "Good. I want the suspense to be driving you crazy by the time we get there."

I wasn't going to let that happen. I changed the subject. "Have you decided where you're going to go to college this fall?"

"Alabama."

"Do you know what you want to major in?"

"Not really. What about you?"

"Pre-law, Samford University."

"Oh yeah," he said. "You told me that before, didn't you?"

I nodded and wrapped my arms around myself to try to get warm.

He turned right into a fancy subdivision. "Have you figured it out yet?"

"A party at someone's house?"

He tilted his head to the side. "How about a party at *my* house?" He made a few turns and pulled into the driveway of a brick house with stonework and black shutters.

"This is your house?"

"Yeah."

The home had to be at least five thousand square feet with an immaculate lawn and gardens around the porch and entryway. "Wow! It's stunning."

"My parents' house," he amended. He parked the car. "Come on, let me show you around."

He gave me a brief tour of their home. It had an open floor plan with four bedrooms, huge windows, a pool in the back, and a spacious kitchen with granite countertops. Everything gleamed.

I leaned against the island and asked, "When do you expect the others to show up?"

"What others?"

"For the party."

He laughed. "It's a *private party*. Just you and me."

I gave him a confused look.

"My parents and Maura went out this evening. We have the whole place to ourselves, until nine-thirty anyhow."

I stared at him. The silence spun out. I smiled nervously. "Great."

"You want something to drink?" he asked. "A wine cooler, maybe, or a beer…"

"Um." Did I really want to drink alcohol with him tonight, alone, here at his parent's house? I might relax—too much. But what if *I* was the problem in our relationship? What if drinking would help me relax and take the stick out of my butt. Might things become better between us?

"Come on," he said. "Live a little."

I pulled out one of the tall chairs and sat at the island. "I don't really drink. What do you have?"

"Let's take a look." He opened the giant stainless steel refrigerator. He listed a few types of drinks, but the one that sounded best was a type of hard lemonade. How bad could lemonade be?

"Okay, I'll try that one."

He pulled a bottle from the refrigerator and handed it to me. He chose a beer for himself.

"Won't your parents notice?" I asked. "I mean, don't they count?"

"No, they trust me. Besides, we're not going to drink them *all*—are we? I mean, you're not a closet alcoholic or something, are you?"

"No, not at all. I'll be lucky to drink this one. I don't want to get sick."

"One won't make you sick. Now, four or five of them… maybe." He grinned.

"You'd have to scrape me off the floor if I drank that many."

"I'll keep an eye on you, then. Make sure you don't sneak out here and raid the refrigerator."

"You don't have to worry about that."

He raised his eyebrows. "Do you want to go into the living room? We can watch a movie or something."

"Sure."

I followed him through a hall that ran parallel to the stairs leading to the second floor. Pictures of Brody and his family hung on the walls. Their home was really lovely.

"Your mom is a really good interior decorator," I said. "I love these frames she's using."

We stopped in the hallway to look at the pictures.

"She loves this stuff," Brody said. "Dad's always complaining about her shopping for the house."

"Is this you when you were a baby?"

He rolled his eyes. "Yes. And that one."

"You were so cute."

He made a groaning noise in his throat and rolled his eyes, embarrassed. "Come on!"

We went into the living room. Brody reached for the remote. "What are you in the mood for? We have everything."

I sipped from the bottle. My drink tasted sour, like lemonade and something else. Not as horrible as I thought it would be, actually. Kind of good. It went down easy.

I walked over to the wall containing their DVD collection. He was right; they had an impressive selection of movies to choose from.

"Lots of animated movies," I noted.

"Maura is only eight, remember."

"Right. There's also lots of Batman, Superman, Spiderman, Ironman…"

"Who doesn't like those?"

"It would be un-American," I agreed. "Romantic comedy, dramas, horror…"

He came up behind me and put his hands on my hips. "Horror. You might have to cuddle up to me for protection."

"Mmm." I selected a movie and pulled it off the shelf.

"*The Incredibles.*" He frowned. "I figured you for a romantic comedy girl."

"This has it all: humor, family fun, evil villain, and superheroes."

"If you say so." He released me.

"You've never watched it?" I turned to look at him, surprised.

"It's one of Maura's movies."

I waved the DVD in the air. "Oh no, there's plenty of goodness here for everyone."

He looked at the drink in my hand. "Are you ready for another yet?"

"No, just one for me."

"You need to drink faster." He slid the movie into the player.

Why?

I sat on the couch, and Brody joined me, sitting so close that our legs were tight against one another. I put my bottle on a coaster. It was three-quarters empty, and I vowed to stop drinking the rest of it. My head seemed to be buzzing already, and a long movie was about to begin. The last thing I wanted was to fall asleep on his couch. How embarrassing would that be?

Brody put a hand on my leg, mid-thigh. The movie began to play. With his left hand, Brody ran the remote to fast-forward through the opening credits, and with his right, he moved his hand around on my leg, massaging. It crossed my mind that maybe I should feel nervous about being alone here with him. The drink had begun to settle into my blood, and it worked its intended magic, making me feel relaxed, weightless, and slow.

On the screen, cartoon characters started moving and talking. We watched for about ten minutes before Brody put his drink on a coaster and shifted toward me. Lowering his head toward my ear, he whispered, "You drive me crazy, you know that?"

"I do?" I murmured.

"You're so hot." He turned toward me and began kissing me. In the car he usually began with soft kissing, but this time, his hands reached for either side of my head and pulled me roughly against him. His long fingers wound into my hair. His lips and tongue ground against mine. After a few seconds of that, he pushed me backwards into the cushions, and the weight of him made me feel like I was being smothered. The cloying smell of his cologne filled my nostrils. Decorative pillows hemmed me in on either side. Brody's hands reached beneath my shirt and squeezed my breasts through my bra, painfully. I could hardly breathe.

He thrust against me, and I could feel the hardness of him through his jeans, and I became afraid. My head cleared in an instant. I was alone at this boy's house, and no one knew where I was. I pushed helplessly against his shirtfront.

He didn't stop. Without lifting his mouth from mine, his hands traveled across my belly, toward the waistline of my jeans.

I bucked my hips, trying to unseat him from my body. I felt very small and weak, a hundred and nine pounds of nothing against his muscle. Where was the scrappy tomboy I used to be? Where was she when I really needed her?

Terror made me strong, but not strong enough. Brody's fingers began trying to loosen the button of my jeans, and I turned my face, gasping. "No, no, I don't want this!"

"Olivia, calm down," he murmured. "I'm just kissing you."

"No, stop it!"

He yanked at my jeans, which stubbornly refused to unhook, thank goodness. While he was distracted, I jammed my bony knee into the soft spot of his thigh.

"Ow! Crap, Olivia, that hurt!" It caught him off guard. He rolled off me, and I flung myself off the couch. I jumped to my feet and put some furniture between us.

Breathing hard, I backed away from him. "Why did you do that? I said no!"

"I didn't do anything!" He scowled at me and tossed his bangs away from his eyes with a shake of his head.

I stared at him, furious and hurt. "That's it, that's all you ever wanted from me, isn't it?"

"You are so naïve, you know that?" He hit the stop button on the movie. "Grow up. Try watching a few adult movies."

Tears blurred my vision. This was it. Brody and I were breaking up. I wasn't sure if we'd ever technically been boyfriend and girlfriend because we'd only gone on a couple of dates, but whatever we'd had, it was over. I wanted nothing more to do with Brody Tipton.

"I want to go home!" I said.

"Then go." He rubbed his leg and made no move to get off the couch.

"You're not taking me?"

"I'm not taking you anywhere—not home, not to the prom, not anywhere. You can find your own ride. I'm tired of paying for nothing."

I stood there, looking at him. "I don't even know where I am."

He smirked. "I guess you're in a world of hurt, then, aren't you?"

I hated that smirk. What he seemed to forget was that I'd beaten him at mini golf and go-carts. I was smart enough to find my own way home.

"Jerk," I said. I turned, grabbed my purse from the kitchen counter, and left the house. I went down the driveway. I looked at the mailbox: 44164. Okay, but what was the street address? I started walking.

I dug my cell phone out of my purse and prayed that Alice was available. I dialed her number.

"Hello?"

"Thank God you answered!" I said.

"What's wrong?" Her voice was instantly concerned.

"I need you to come get me."

"What happened?"

"I'll explain everything when you get here. Can you come?"

"Where are you?"

I looked around as I walked. "I'm trying to figure that out now."

"Okay, sweetie, you're really starting to scare me."

"Brody," I said.

"What did he do?"

"He got really pushy with me tonight," I said.

"Are you okay? Did he hurt you?" Alice's voice became very quiet, concerned. I knew what she was thinking. We'd heard about a girl from our school a few years ago who *wasn't* okay, who'd been raped at a party one night.

"I'm okay." I looked over my shoulder. No one was following me. I was alone in a high-end subdivision, trying to find my way out so my best friend could look up the address based on the name on the front gate. "He brought me to his parent's house, but all I have is a house number. I'm walking, trying to figure out what subdivision I'm in. You're going to need to look up the address."

"What's the street name for the house?"

"I don't know. I haven't reached the end of the street yet."

"He wouldn't even take you home?"

My throat burned, but I refused to cry over him. Not here. I was going to stay strong. "It was a bad breakup," I said. "Bad."

I came to the end of his parents' street. Ahead, I could also see the entrance to the subdivision with a sign.

"The street is Hinkle Court. The subdivision entrance is just ahead, but I can't read the sign yet."

"Give me a house number. I can find you from the street name, I think."

I gave her the number of the house to my right and kept walking toward the sign.

"Okay," Alice said. "I can be there in fifteen minutes. Hang tight."

"Okay, thanks."

I hung up and kept walking toward the sign. The events of the past two hours kept playing in my head like a bad movie. The reality of what might have happened to me became clear, although aside from refusing the drink, I wasn't sure what I could have done to avoid the situation. When we left the school, I had no idea that he'd planned to take me to a house without adults.

I thought about his rough hands, squeezing, pushing, and his lips crushing mine. I didn't feel lucky anymore.

I went to the sign and hid, afraid suddenly that Brody might change his mind and come after me. My head was spinning from the drink I'd had, though I hadn't drunk enough to feel too much effect. It was probably my lack of food. I felt cold. The night seemed very dark. To defend myself, I picked up a brick I found lying loose in the bushes—just in case.

108/ 100

April 24

On Friday morning, everything was different, and nothing was different. The scale said I'd lost another pound. I ran hill sprints and ate a single hard-boiled egg for breakfast. Those things stayed the same.

After first period, Brody didn't stop at my locker to say hello. That was different.

At lunch, I felt too upset to be hungry. That was different, too. Hunger had been such a constant these past few weeks that its absence was more noticeable than Brody's. I stared at my banana and said nothing while Alice and Nash tried to cheer me up with a spirited round of Brody bashing. Part of me wanted to participate, especially after the way he had treated me, but the other part was hurt and confused. I felt raw.

A huge banner above the far door announced the theme for this year's prom, which was just one week away. No prom for me, not now.

Losing weight for the prom, buying a dress for the prom, dating Brody before the prom—my whole life for these past two months had been wrapped up with this big event, and now I wasn't even going. It wasn't fair. Why? Because I didn't want to have sex with Brody Tipton?

"He was a terrible kisser," I said, contributing to the bashing. "For the record."

Alice laughed. "You never told me that!"

"It never came up. But he is."

Alice and Nash looked at one another. I was afraid that they might start kissing right here in the lunchroom. If so, I might puke.

"I can't believe you're not going to the prom," Alice said. "After buying that fabulous dress and *everything*. He's such a huge butt-wipe."

I agreed. However, I didn't want to feel even sadder about not going to the prom, so I said, "It's just a dance. In the end."

"*Homecoming* is just a dance. The prom is *The Prom*."

I knew she was right. The prom was Cinderella's ball. It was every romantic cotillion ever filmed. Every single girl was beautiful at the prom. Love was possible for anyone. Magic happened there.

I still wanted to go.

"I have a cousin that you could ask," Nash suggested. "He's not much of a looker, but he can drive."

"I'm *not* asking your cousin to the prom," I snapped.

He looked hurt, and I regretted my snippiness.

"I'm sorry, Nash," I said. "I know you're just trying to help."

"Oh, I know. You should ask that guy you work with!" Alice said. "What's his name?"

"Ross?"

"Yeah, him."

My heart sped up, but I shook my head. "He's just a friend."

"You hang out almost every weekend. I bet he'd go with you if you asked."

"The prom's next week. He probably couldn't get a tux on such short notice."

"Sure he could," Nash said. "Unless he's some weird size."

I scrunched up my face. "I just don't feel right about it. I mean, he knows about Brody asking me to the prom and that we've been dating, and he'd know that he'd just be... you know, like second string."

"You should ask anyway," Alice insisted. "I want you to go. And you still want to go, too. I know you do. We were going to have so much fun together." She made a pouty face.

Ross *would* like Alice and Nash. I knew we'd all have a good time at the prom together. But asking Ross just seemed wrong. I liked him too much to make him feel like my second choice.

"I do, but I can't do that to him."

At the end of our shift at the diner, Ross and I cleaned up together. The whole time, I kept thinking about Alice's suggestion. Whenever I thought he wasn't looking, I watched him and imagined him taking me into his strong arms for a slow dance. The idea sent funny flip-flops through my insides.

We mopped the bakery and kitchen floors and then carried the trash to the dumpster out back. In between tossing the heavy bags into the bin, he asked, "You still want to go riding on Sunday afternoon?"

I bit my lip. "I don't know if I'll be good company this weekend."

"You haven't been much company *tonight*. I can tell you're in a funk about something. What's wrong?"

"Brody and I broke up last night."

"Jeez."

I nodded.

He tossed another bag. "Isn't your prom tomorrow night?"

"Next Saturday. Looks like I'm not going to the prom after all."

It was a perfect opportunity to ask him. All I had to do was remind him about that amazing red dress that needed to be worn and what a shame it would be to leave it in the closet. I was pretty sure that he'd say yes. We were friends.

But what if he said no? After what happened with Brody, I couldn't face any more rejection and pain. I just couldn't.

"This might sound selfish, but I'm relieved," he said.

I smiled in the dark, thinking that he was also contemplating my newfound singleness. "Why's that?"

"Because now you can stop dieting. You don't need to lose any more weight to please Brody before the prom or to compete with his ex-girlfriend or anything like that."

My smile vanished, but I covered my disappointment with an attempt at humor. "I guess you're right," I said. "Lose a boyfriend, gain a cheeseburger."

I threw the last bag into the dumpster, and we headed toward the diner.

104 / 100

April 30

One of the best things about my mom was her willingness to give me space. Nana and Pappy had meddled enough in her business growing up—even reading her diary—that she'd gone the other way with her parenting. As long as I kept my grades up and my nose clean, she left me alone.

Until Thursday evening, when she knocked on my door, once, and then walked in without waiting for me to invite her.

I put my book aside and sat up on my bed. "What?"

She came over and stood beside me, looking intently at me, searching. I felt like she could see into my brain and knew what was happening to me.

"What?" I repeated.

"Want to order pizza for dinner?"

Before my diet, eating together had been a common bonding activity for us. I ran so much that I didn't gain weight, even with the fatty, high-calorie foods that she loved.

"I already ate," I lied.

"What did you eat?"

"Soup."

She sighed. She sat on the edge of the bed and reached out to brush my hair behind my ear. "Olivia…"

I was glad that I was wearing my baggiest sweats. I had been cold when I got home from practice tonight. I was always cold, and I'd wanted to put something heavy and thick on my body. Layers stood between my bones and her seeking eyes.

I swallowed and pulled my knees to my chest. "What's wrong, Mom?"

"I'm concerned about you."

"I'm fine."

"You don't need to lose any more weight."

"I'm not. I'm maintaining."

She shook her head. "Just this past week, you look like you've dropped another ten pounds."

Only five. I squeezed my knees even tighter. My body felt hollow and brittle. "Brody and I broke up," I confided. "He's not taking me to the prom."

"Oh, honey. I'm so sorry."

She looked like she wanted to hug me, which would be a terrible thing because then she'd feel my body. I stayed in a tight ball with my arms wrapped around my knees.

"It's for the best," I said. "We really weren't that good for each other."

She stroked my hair. "That explains why you've been hiding away up here all week."

"Yeah."

She sighed. "I remember what it felt like, breaking up. It was the worst feeling in the world."

I thought about what it must have been like for her when Dad left. I nodded. "Yeah."

Had she ever had to fight off someone who got too frisky on the couch and tried to smother her with toothy kisses? Had she ever found herself pinned beneath a heavy body, beneath someone who was hurting her, who didn't even ask whether or not she wanted his hands invading places they hadn't been invited to explore? Was that a terrifying rite of passage that every girl had to experience?

"But honey," she said, "you can't starve yourself. He's not worth it."

"I'm not! I eat. You see me eat."

"I see you eat a single hard-boiled egg. Or a can of soup."

"That's not starving. And I told you before that I'm maintaining my weight now, not losing. I eat other things now like fruit, yogurt, even some chicken at school. I eat *healthy* things."

She sighed. "You're not eating enough. You're too thin."

"Mom, I know you love me. I love you, too. But I'm eighteen, an adult, and able to make my own decisions about my body weight. I'm telling you that I'm fine."

We looked at one another. Since the last time she'd questioned my diet, we'd stayed far away from this subject. It was dangerous territory for both of us.

"You might be legally an adult," she said, "but you're still my child. And I'm worried about you. I don't want you to lose any more weight."

"I won't." I gave her my most winning smile. "I promise. I already told you that."

"You're *really* not dieting anymore?"

She gave me such an earnest expression that I almost wanted to tell her everything. My whole life had spun out of control, and I didn't know how to fix it anymore.

I shook my head. "No, Mom."

"How about that pizza, then? One slice?"

I shrugged and conceded. "All right. Thin crust."

She smiled. "I can do that."

I smiled, too.

"You want to come downstairs and play Yahtzee?" she asked.

"Maybe after the pizza comes, okay?"

"Sure."

She stood. I watched her leave. Mom's soft roundness seemed familiar and wonderful. How could I love her just the way she was but hate myself so much—hate my fat?

I logged onto my computer and went to the Blubber Busters site.

Olivia: 5'4", 104 / 100: Help! My mom's about to make me eat pizza. I insisted on thin crust, but that's the only thing I knew to do. Any tips before it gets here?

Jane: 5'4", 93 / 100: Purge.

Jane was the same height as me. She was the one I'd been thinking about when I changed my goal weight from one hundred and ten pounds to one hundred. I was now only four pounds away from my new goal, and she was at ninety-three. I wondered what I'd look like at ninety-three. What did she look like at that weight? Was there a dress size smaller than zero?

Jane's advice sounded disgusting. I didn't want to vomit pizza.

Dana: 5'7", 145 / 125: Eat one piece, very slowly, and drink lots of water. Try to avoid a binge.

Molly: 5'0", 114 / 90: Eat salad or something healthy with the pizza so you're not starving. That will help you stick to just one piece. And lots of water.

Jane: 5'4", 93 / 100: Just purge.

I squinted at her picture. Jane looked like a wisp of a girl, very pretty and delicate. How recent was that photo?

Olivia: 5'4", 104 / 100: Thanks for all the tips, everyone. I don't know what I'd do without the support of these boards.

I logged out. I got up and walked over to my closet. The clear plastic enveloping my prom dress hissed at me as I reached for my slippers. I looked at the red gown and thought about Alice's suggestion to ask Ross to the prom. I still had time. If I asked him tomorrow night, maybe he would have enough time to get something to wear.

The thing was, I no longer thought he'd say yes. I'd told him that Brody and I broke up, and since then, we'd worked together on Saturday night and rode together on Sunday. Neither of us mentioned the prom or Brody. If Ross had any interest in me or in going to the prom with me, I would have known, but I didn't think he did. Nothing had changed between us now that I was "single" again.

104.5 / 100

May 1

On Friday morning, the scale judged me for eating that slice of thin-crust pizza, and the result was that I gained a half pound. I shouldn't have done it. Or, I should have followed Jane's advice and purged. *Fat*, the scale said. *Weak. Fail.*

I skipped breakfast.

In my morning classes, I doodled pictures of skinny silhouettes in my notebook. I didn't see Brody at all. It was as if we'd never been an item at all. I'd dreamed him.

When I met Alice for lunch, she was alone. "We have to talk," she said.

I knew this wasn't going anywhere good. "About what?"

"Come on, get a tray." Her chunky turquoise watch rattled against the plastic as she picked one up for herself.

I joined her in the cafeteria line. "Where's Nash?"

"Sitting with other friends today. I told him I was doing an intervention with you."

"An intervention about what?" I gave her a funny look and stifled a laugh.

"It's not funny, Olivia." Her eyes watered and threatened to wash away all that black mascara and eyeliner. "You look *terrible*. You need help."

She was just jealous because I was skinny, and she wasn't. "I'm fine."

"You're not fine!" People were looking at us, and she lowered her voice to a whisper. "When we went dress shopping, you *promised me* that you'd stop dieting, but you haven't. You've lost something like thirty pounds in two months, when you didn't even need to lose any weight to begin with. You're an anorexic."

"I'm *not* an anorexic! I eat. And I don't throw up or anything like that."

"I don't believe you," she said, shaking her head and sending her dangling earrings into a spinning, sparkling dance. She swallowed and seemed to get herself under control. "And anyway, regardless of how you've done it, you've gone too far. You look *sick*. What does your mother say?"

Sick? I shoved my tray along the rail. "For your information, Mom and I ate pizza together last night. You can call her and ask if you don't believe me."

She gave me a skeptical look.

"I don't need an intervention," I said. "I eat."

"Not enough."

I thought about the hard-boiled eggs, bananas, and chicken soup that I ate one small bite at a time for dinner. True, I didn't eat a lot of these things anymore, not like I did in the beginning when I started with Boot Camp, but I didn't starve completely. I needed energy to race.

We reached the food part of the cafeteria line, and Alice put several items on my tray. "All I see you eat are bananas, maybe a cup of yogurt or soup. Today, you're going to have a real meal like the rest of us."

I stared at the mound of food. I resented her pushiness. I wasn't *sick*. "I can't eat all that."

"It's what every other student is having for lunch."

"It's too much. I had pizza last night."

"So you said. Come on, do your best." Alice walked toward the cashier, and I followed, carrying the tray of food, my mouth watering despite myself. I couldn't remember the last time I'd had tater tots and battered fish. February?

We checked out and found a table by ourselves. It was nice that I didn't have to share Alice with Nash for once, even if she was scolding me.

I picked up a tater tot. "I don't appreciate being told that I look terrible and sick," I said. "I've worked really hard to lose some weight."

Alice sighed. Her gaze softened. "Sweetie, I'm sorry. I didn't mean to hurt your feelings."

"I just wanted to look beautiful for the prom." It was my turn to get teary-eyed.

"You're already beautiful."

I thought about the day when Brody asked me to the prom and my curly fries and how he'd essentially told me that I was too fat. Blaming him for all of this would be easy. He was a big jerk. He'd taken my low self-esteem and combined it with my jealousy and competitiveness with Erica Miller to create a monster.

Except I let him, didn't I? I was the one who'd gone on the diet—and stuck to it.

And now that I wasn't competing with Erica Miller, nor going to the prom, what reason did I have to continue dieting? Personal best on the scale? To beat a girl named Jane, who I didn't even know?

I decided to come clean with Alice. She was my best friend, after all.

"There's something I never told you," I said. I popped the tater tot in my mouth and chewed. It tasted salty and good. My stomach perked up, and I grabbed another.

"What?"

"On the day when Brody asked me to the prom, he said something to me. He told me that he asked me early so I had 'a couple of months to lose a little weight.' I guess that's how all of this started."

Her eyes bulged.

"I figured that he was right, you know," I said, "that I was fat—at least compared to other girls, the type of girls that he liked to date. And I wanted to be his type of girl."

"Are you kidding me?"

"It worked. The thinner I became, the more attention he paid to me. Within two weeks of my diet, he asked me out on a real date, not just for the prom. He treated me like he wanted me to be his girlfriend."

"You were never fat, Olivia."

"He made me feel like I was, though. And now, I like being thin. I like the way my body feels. Well, most of the time. I miss being strong and being able to run far and fast. But maybe I don't need that anymore."

"You've always raced. In fact, I thought you wanted to be on the team in college?"

"Maybe, maybe not. High school is over. Maybe in college, I should be someone different than the athletic tomboy. College is a chance to change who I am."

"Why would you want to do that? Don't you *like* who you are?"

I shrugged. "Sometimes I'm not really sure who I am, or what I want."

"You're a champion."

"Because my brother is."

"Your brother hasn't been in this school for six years. It's just been *you*... running, winning. *You* are the champion."

"But I've done so poorly this year."

"Because of this stupid diet! Gain some weight and start eating again, and you'll go back to being the winner that you've always been."

I looked at my plate. I'd eaten half of the tater tots and about three nibbles of the fish. None of the coleslaw or corn.

"It's so hard," I said.

She noticed my line of sight. "You have to eat more than that."

"I've already eaten so much more than I normally do."

"Try the coleslaw."

"I don't like coleslaw. And I'm not a child, Alice. I can figure out how to feed myself."

"Apparently not. Eat your roll, then. Everyone likes bread."

I picked up the roll and tore it in half. "Thanks for talking to me. I do feel better."

"I'm your best friend. You can always talk to me."

Friday night at the diner was as chaotic as ever. "I need platters," Sally yelled as soon as I walked in the door.

"Why don't you just ask Mr. Lee to order more, so you don't run out every week?" I grabbed a bin and began loading the dishwasher.

"Why don't you get here faster?"

"Because I'm *in school*," I reminded her for the hundredth time.

She danced behind the steam table with a smile on her face.

Ross walked out of the cooler with a tray of battered catfish fillets. "Hey, Olivia."

"Hi, wow. How long have you been here?" I asked, pushing the plastic rack into the machine.

"Fifteen minutes."

"You're already filthy." He even had flour in his hair—and on his eyebrows.

"Nancy quit," he said. "We're short a waitress tonight. It's your big chance."

"Her big chance for what?" Sally asked. She spun a pirouette between the grill and the fryers.

"Oh no," I said. "Not on a Friday night."

"Be courageous. You can do it."

I thought about my talk with Alice today. She called me a champion. Champions weren't afraid to take risks.

Was that who I was?

"Who will wash dishes?" I asked.

"What are the two of you talking about?" Sally asked.

Ross gave me the look. I sighed. "I've been thinking about trying the waitressing job," I told Sally. "I'd like to try some shifts this summer. Ross is suggesting that since we're short-handed, tonight might be the right time to ask Mr. Lee—"

"No way, I need her back here!" Sally said, her eyes looking at someone behind me.

"Go," Mr. Lee said. "I'll take dishes."

I spun around, heart thumping. "Really? Right now?"

"There's an extra apron under the front counter. Ask Tiffany to help you out."

"Are you sure?" I stammered. "I mean…"

"You've been working here for more than a year. You know how it's done, and I need someone with experience. Go."

I met Ross's eyes. He winked and gave me a thumbs up. Mr. Lee grabbed the bus tub and began clearing dishes. Yes, this was what I wanted. I could do this. I scurried to the front counter and looked for the spare apron.

"I'm helping out," I said to Tiffany when she came to the coffee machine. "Where do you want me?"

"Take the booths along the wall. The couple in the back just sat down. One unsweet, one water."

I fixed the drinks and hurried to the table to take the orders. It went a lot easier than I expected. Mr. Lee was right; I *did* know how things worked around here, and I quickly fell into a rhythm. It didn't go without a couple of mistakes. I brought someone regular fries instead of sweet potato fries one time, for example.

At the end of the shift, I was exhausted but happy as I counted my tips.

"Thank you," I said to Mr. Lee. "I appreciate the opportunity to try waitressing."

"I'll give you more shifts when school lets out, if you want them," he said.

"Yes, absolutely!"

I helped Tiffany vacuum the dining room and cleaned at the front counter while Ross and Sally handled the kitchen. I refilled salt and pepper shakers. At closing time, I met Ross in the parking lot.

"How did it go?" He stood close to me, his chin tilting down toward my face.

"Crazy busy," I said. "But exhilarating too. Did you miss me in the kitchen?"

"Absolutely. Sally was a bear. She even growled at Mr. Lee."

I laughed. "Thanks for encouraging me. I don't know if I would have jumped in there without your nudge."

"I'm surprised that you don't have more self-confidence, Olivia. You're obviously smart and capable. Everything you touch is gold."

I ducked my head, blushing. He always had that effect on me. "I don't know. I have this critic in my head that keeps saying *you can't* or *you're not good enough*. I guess I listen to it too much."

"Stop it," he commanded in that deep voice of his.

A shiver ran through me. I'd had such a great evening that my courage rose up inside of me again. "So what are you doing tomorrow?" I asked. If he was free, I would ask him to the prom. I would just do it, right now, before I lost my nerve. I would finally act on this intense attraction.

"We're going caving. My group is taking a trip into Georgia for a hiking, camping, caving excursion. We're driving up tomorrow morning, doing the cave, then spending the night, and coming back in the morning. Don't worry, though, I'll be back in time for our regular time on Sunday afternoon."

I paused. "That sounds like fun."

"Yeah, we've been planning it for awhile. What are *you* doing tomorrow—besides working?"

I didn't correct him. He obviously didn't remember that it was my prom night and that I wasn't working because I'd asked for the night off weeks ago. "Nothing. Just hanging out."

"That's cool."

We looked at one another. After a moment, I shrugged and said, "Well, see you here on Sunday afternoon, I guess."

"Yeah. Wish me luck."

"You don't need luck. You have a guide, right?"

"Never leave the surface without one."

On the drive home, I clenched the steering wheel with both hands and tried not to cry. I'd almost asked him. I was so glad that I hadn't embarrassed myself by asking before he had a chance to make the excuses. That would have been humiliating.

103 / 100

May 2

On prom night, I sipped a can of chicken broth for dinner and then took a bath to get warm. Settling into the hot water felt heavenly. I sighed with contentment as the heat seeped into my bones and drove away the persistent chill.

Opening my eyes, I stared down the length of my body. My stomach curved inward between my hip bones, which jutted out of the water like pale mountains on either side of the valley. Sucking in my stomach and taking a deep breath exposed most of my rib cage. My legs were stilts. I felt hollow and buoyant, like I could float away.

After soaking for twenty minutes or so, I got out, put on a pair of soft sweats and a hoodie, and went to my room. My dress hung on the back of my closet door, still in its plastic, whispering. Country music played on my iPod playlist.

My phone buzzed with another text message from Alice, who'd arrived at the school with Nash.

Alice: I wish you and Ross could have come.

Me: :(Brody there?

Alice: Yes.

Me: Who did he bring?

Alice: Erica M.

Me:

Alice: You okay?

Me: Yes. Stop worrying about me and go have fun.

I put my phone down and sat at the computer. Erica Miller! He'd taken Erica to the prom instead of me. It seemed too much to bear.

I logged into the Blubber Busters site and read group posts for awhile.

Bethany: 5'2", 133 / 101: Jane was sent to an in-patient treatment facility this week. She can't have a laptop or cell phone, but I visited her. She's ninety-one. They're making her eat.

Oh, no. Not Jane! Was she okay? What had happened to her? Being sent to a treatment center meant you were an anorexic, didn't it?

Molly: 5'0", 111 / 90: Treatment sucks. Been there, done that.

Bethany: 5'2", 133 / 101: I'm not going to let it get out of hand like that. I'm going to keep my goals realistic for my height.

Molly: 5'0", 111 / 90: We all say that. But being thin is a like a drug. You can't get enough. You reach your goal, and then you lower your goal because you think a little more won't hurt, then a little more, and a little more, and the next thing you know, you're in a treatment facility.

I tried to imagine what it was like for Jane in the hospital: no scales, no Internet to communicate with us on the boards, no calorie restrictions, no exercise. She must be very sick and weak to be there. Maybe she had an IV for fluids. I felt so bad for her. She must be lonely and sad.

Bethany: 5'2", 133 / 101: That's not going to happen to me.
Molly: 5'0", 111 / 90: You keep telling yourself that.

Was *I* an anorexic? Would I become one if I kept losing weight? Jane wasn't that much different than me. We were the same height, close to the same weight, and now she was in a treatment facility.

Lauren: 5'3.5", 107 / 105: It's never going to happen to me because I can't stop bingeing.

Molly: 5'0", 111 / 90: Everyone binges now and then. You can't help it.

I kept reading posts to try to distract myself from thinking about the prom, but in a way they didn't help because the only reason I cared about dieting was *because* of the prom—and Brody. Before him, I'd never worried about daily weigh-ins or statistics or counting calories. I'd been tough and athletic.

Avoiding food was my only strength now. I could survive on a single hard-boiled egg for breakfast, a banana for lunch, and a bowl of chicken noodle soup for dinner—every day, the same thing. Perhaps I couldn't win races anymore, but I could be as light as air, a hundred pounds and able to circle my wrists with my fingers. That made me *beautiful*, didn't it?

I looked at the posts of these girls who struggled with their weight and self-image. I thought about Jane, who was in a treatment center tonight instead of with her friends, and all because of this quest to lose a few more pounds.

I didn't want that to happen to me.

Why did I even want this goal for myself anymore? Brody gave it to me. He's the one who said I wasn't okay the way I was. Maybe, like everything else he said, it was a lie.

I used to be a strong person. A champion. Maybe I still was. After all, I'd been strong enough to say no when Brody had tried to cross a line of intimacy that I wasn't ready to cross, and I'd figured out how to get myself home when he refused to take me—when I didn't even know where I was. I'd been strong enough to try waitressing on a chaotic Friday night, even though I was scared, and I'd done *well*. I'd even been strong enough to ask Ross to go to the prom with me, or I would have been (I think) if he hadn't already had other plans for tonight.

I was strong enough to quit dieting, too.

I went into my Blubber Busters profile and changed my goal weight from 100 to 115. Then I signed out and went to bed.

103 / 115

May 3

On Sunday afternoon as Ross and I hiked over the eastern side of the green mountain with the GPS, he talked about his Saturday caving trip. He made jokes about his brother, but I didn't have much to say. I still had the post-I-missed-out-on-the-prom blues.

"You're killing me, Olivia. Say something."

"We're never going to find this cave." I sat down on a boulder and dropped my head into my hands.

"We won't with an attitude like that."

"Maybe your grandfather is mis-remembering, and it was another farm and another mountain," I suggested.

Ross sat beside me on the boulder. "He's not senile. If he says it's here, I believe him."

"I'm sorry," I said. Even though I'd eaten something for both breakfast and lunch, I still felt tired and weak, just from walking up and down the hills. I didn't want Ross to know that.

Birds sang around us. A nice breeze rustled the leaves and my hair. It was cooler today than it had been earlier in the week, with lower humidity. The sky was pure blue.

"If you want to stop looking with me, I'll understand," Ross said.

I looked sharply at him. "No! That's not what I meant. I like coming out here with you. I *want* to find it."

"Then what's wrong? You seem really out of it today."

"I guess I don't feel that great. Since the breakup with Brody…" I swallowed. "I haven't been doing so well."

"You liked him a lot, huh?" His question seemed to pain him.

I thought about that a minute, then lowered my head. "No, not really. Not as much as I wanted to. I wanted someone different than he turned out to be."

His expression softened. "Who did you want?"

You.

I shook my head. "It doesn't matter."

"It does. Tell me."

I decided to try and explain. "My best friend and her boyfriend have been dating for three years. You should see how they are together. They're…" I gestured with my hands.

"Nauseating?"

"Exactly! And yet wonderful at the same time. It makes me so jealous sometimes. Their loving glances, their tender little notes to each other, that dreamy look that Nash gives Alice sometimes… It probably sounds stupid, but I want what they have. I want to be held. I want to be taken care of, sometimes. I want to have someone who consumes my thoughts, who makes me laugh until my sides ache, who kisses me like—" I stopped.

Ross stared at me intently. "Go on, like what?"

I swallowed. "Who can kiss me like I'm his cherished sweetheart, and then who can also kiss me passionately without trying to eat my face off."

He laughed.

"It's not funny," I insisted, my own mouth twitching toward a smile.

"It's a little bit funny."

"Chemistry is an important component to a relationship."

He nodded, blinking those hazel eyes at me. "I agree a hundred percent. Chemistry."

The breeze picked up some of his wild brown curls and tossed them around his face. My fingers itched to brush them away.

"I want someone who gets me," I murmured. "That's an important part of it, too."

"A soul mate?"

"It's not as corny as it sounds."

"I didn't say it was," he said. "I believe in soul mates, too."

"You do?"

"I like a good love story. I even read them occasionally."

I sighed. "Then you know. *That's* what I want."

"But Olivia, those are novels. Real love is messier. You know that, right?"

"What I know is that sometimes what you thought was love really isn't. Dads leave their families and never come back. Guys ask you to the prom and then they—"

"So you're saying that if people let you down, then it's not real love?"

I shrugged. "I don't know, maybe."

"Sometimes people hurt the people they love. That doesn't mean they don't love them."

I squinted at him. "I just don't want to be hurt again."

His deep voice became quiet. "I don't want to hurt you."

We stared at one another. I kept waiting for him to lean forward and kiss me, but he didn't. He just gazed at me, his eyes darkening.

After a long moment, I decided to take matters into my own hands. I leaned forward and stretched my hand out to touch those curls that had been distracting me for weeks. So soft! I brushed them a few times, felt them run through the webbing between my fingers, and tucked a few strands behind his ear. Ross didn't move, didn't even seem to breathe. With my own heart pounding, I let my hand trail down the side of his face, along the question mark scar, and to his shirt collar. My thumb and index finger rubbed the material a minute, deciding.

Staring at his lips, I tugged gently, and he obliged. We met in the middle. Our mouths touched, and I continued drawing closer, crawling across the rock until I was half sitting on his lap, my arms wrapping around his shoulders and pulling him even closer. His tongue felt soft and warm, searching instead of demanding. Desire raced through my veins. I deepened the kiss. I felt every inch of his body pressing against mine and all the sensations coursing through my own.

Leisurely, I pulled my lips away from his, rubbed noses, and arched back to look into his eyes.

I raised my eyebrows, wondering.

"I feel like you just tried to eat my face off," Ross said, deadpan.

"Seriously."

He squeezed me tighter against him. "I am the happiest guy in the whole world."

I rubbed my nose again with his and lowered my face, feeling shy. "Me too."

"So now what?"

I thought about more kissing. "I don't know."

"There's something I've been wanting to ask you for a long time, actually. Maybe this means that you'll say yes."

I leaned back and looked at him, immensely curious.

"Will you go to the prom with me? It's next weekend at my school."

I stared at him, open-mouthed.

"Or not… I mean, if you don't want to," he said. "I just thought, since you bought a dress and everything, and you wanted a romantic night with a fancy dinner and a guy in a tux and—"

"Yes."

"I was getting worried there for a minute."

"It's this coming Saturday?" I asked.

"Yes."

I smiled. "I am so going to kiss you again."

"You do what you have to do."

I took a breath, leaned forward, and pressed my lips against his. He waited, as if taking cues from me. I wouldn't want that forever, but right now I liked that he let me lead the way. It felt powerful. I opened my mouth to his, and he responded by tightening his arms around me.

I pushed him so that he lay flat on the rock, and I stretched on top of him. I kissed him over and over. Nothing about kissing Ross felt bad. It wasn't scary or boring or slobbery—just amazing. He ran his hands up and down my back, staying in safe zones, and I liked that, for now. He understood. Somehow, he got me. I kissed his neck. It tasted salty from our hike. He sighed and kind of moaned.

"Am I hurting you? Am I too heavy?" I asked, thinking of my weight pressing him into the hard rock.

"You don't weigh anything at all."

I smiled down at him and tucked my hair behind my ear. I liked being a feather on his chest.

He gave me that crooked, goofy grin. "Am I kissing you right?" he asked.

"Definitely."

"I'm giving it my very best."

"You're doing very well," I said. "But I think we shouldn't overdo it on the first try." I rolled off and sat up.

"Are you sure?" he asked.

"No, but I stand by my decision." I stood and tried to dust off my jeans. I turned in a slow circle and spotted something. "Oh my! Ross, look at this! Is that what I think it is?"

He sat up. "What?"

"Come here, come here!"

I pointed at the area nestled between the rocks, which we would have spotted if we had walked three more feet to the left before taking our break. A thicket of brush surrounded the dark hole.

Ross pulled back some of the bushes. There it was. A small cave entrance, big enough for a person to crawl into and hold their knees to their chest, with a narrow passageway that disappeared into darkness. I felt a surge of excitement.

"We found it, didn't we? This is it!" I said.

He nodded, grinning. "This is it."

He went on his hands and knees and approached the cave.

"Don't!" I said. "What if there are spiders?"

He laughed. "There probably are." He pulled away the brush and looked inside. "This is so awesome." He crawled forward.

"You said you didn't go in without a guide," I reminded him.

"I'm not going far."

Soon his calves and shoes were the only things sticking out of the hole.

"Ross, I mean it." I grabbed his legs. "I don't know how to find my way out of the woods if you get stuck and need help. You can't do this."

He began backing out of the cave. "Don't worry, I can't see much anyway. But it's a good cave, a passable entrance."

He grinned at me and stood. Then he picked me up and spun around.

"We did it!" he said.

"We did, didn't we?"

206

He lowered me to the ground, pulled out a notepad that he'd been carrying in his pocket, and looked at his GPS. He wrote down the coordinates, and then he used his phone to take pictures. He snapped one of me.

"Stop it," I said, smiling.

"And you thought it was hopeless. 'We're never going to find this cave,' you said. And it was right here, all along."

Just like Ross—right here all along.

105 / 115

May 9

Saturday afternoon, a week later, found me sitting on a stool in front of Alice, watching in the bathroom mirror while she brushed, braided, and curled my hair into something fabulous for Ross's prom. She'd chosen to leave it long and elegant, with everything swept over my left shoulder and falling into a mass of large curls. A single braid wove over my head like a rope and held everything in place.

The girl looking back at me in the mirror seemed like a stranger. Smoky brown eyes, red lipstick, chiseled cheekbones, and that gorgeous hair. Who was she? Where was the muscular tomboy in the ponytail and sweat pants?

"How do you know when you're in love?" I asked.

Alice giggled. "Trust me, you just know."

"What was it about Nash?"

"Being with him, I guess. When we first met, I couldn't get enough of his presence, his laugh, the sound of his voice. I wanted to spend every moment with him, and I didn't care what we did."

"Plus, he's so romantic," I pointed out.

"He is," she agreed. "I love his sweet little gifts and the way he acts so chivalrous around me, opening doors and stuff like that, but that's just a small part of the package. It's *him*. It's spending time with him."

"I *thought* I was in love with Brody, but looking back, I think I was only in love with the *idea* of being in love with him."

I closed my eyes, remembering his pawing hands and wet lips. He wasn't anything that I thought he was.

"I feel so stupid," I said. "Tammy warned me about him. You did, too."

"Neither of us warned you he was like *that*. None of us had any idea he'd turn out to be that way."

I watched her work for a few minutes.

"I wanted to fall in love with someone this year," I said, "like you."

"What about this Ross guy?"

"I love hanging out with him. We spend hours together and never get tired of talking. Sometimes it's like he can read my mind, you know? He cracks me up at work all the time. He's great. And last weekend when we kissed, there was *definitely* chemistry! Totally different from kissing Brody."

"But you're not sure whether or not you're in love with him?" She raised her eyebrows.

I blushed. "I think I am."

She put the brush on the counter and placed her hands on my shoulders. "Then I definitely need to meet this guy and make sure I approve."

Our eyes met in the mirror. "I can't believe how beautiful you made me look."

"You *are* beautiful." She squeezed and released my shoulders. "Now go put on that dress and let's see the total package. He's going to be here soon, and your mom's going to want a ton of pictures."

I went into my bedroom and changed into my prom gown and strappy red shoes. I'd lost weight since I'd bought it, so the fitted bodice and tight hips weren't nearly as snug as it had been in the store. I modeled the red, floor-length dress for myself in the mirror. My left leg—pencil-thin now—showed through a slit up the thigh. Spinning around to admire the backless view and little train off the end of the skirt, I also noticed that my bubble butt had vanished.

Blubber Busters had helped me accomplish my goal of getting super skinny for the prom, only I wasn't healthy now. I might have the body of a high-fashion underwear model, but I couldn't run distance or win races anymore. I'd lost something of myself to get here—for a jerk who didn't even matter. The price for this look was too high.

The image in the mirror made me think about Jane. How was she doing? She'd been one of my biggest supporters and virtual friends on this journey, and I missed her voice on the boards. I hoped she was getting well. I wished for wellness for both of us.

I opened the bedroom door and went downstairs to the living room, twirling in the center of the floor.

"Oh, honey!" Mom said. "I love the dress on you. And I love what Alice did with your hair."

"That dress totally rocks," Alice agreed. "I forgot how great it looked on you."

"I feel like a tango dancer," I said.

A car pulled into the driveway. I heard the door slam and felt my heart rate take off.

"Let me get my camera," Mom said, and she dashed into the kitchen.

A moment later, the doorbell rang. Alice answered it. "You must be Ross," she said. "I'm Alice, the BFF. I've heard tons about you. Nice to finally meet and greet."

"Same here."

She opened the door wider, and Ross stepped into the foyer. He wore a black tux with a red cummerbund that matched my dress. He held a clear plastic box with a rose corsage.

"You look beautiful, Olivia," he said.

"Thanks." I felt my cheeks heating up. "You look pretty good yourself."

He limped toward me, extending the box with outstretched hands, and I met him halfway. The rose was attached to a sprig of baby's breath and a thin band of lace to slip around my wrist.

"Okay, you kids, I want to take some pictures outside where the light's better," Mom said.

I smiled at Ross and rolled my eyes, and we followed her for an amateur photography shoot in front of various landscaping elements in our back yard. The best part was having Ross's arm around my waist, pulling me close, while we smiled for the camera. My dirt bike farm boy looked really hot in his tux, and I suddenly felt shy and eager about the prospect of dancing in his arms. My insides began doing fluttery things.

Mom could have taken pictures all night, so finally I said, "We have to go now. I think you have enough pictures, and there's this dance we're supposed to attend, you know?"

"Okay, okay," she said, laughing. "Go, have fun."

Alice turned sideways so Ross couldn't see her. She gave me two thumbs up and mouthed, "He's cute!"

I nodded and grinned.

"You ready?" he asked.

"Yes, let's get out of here before Mom changes her mind."

He escorted me to the passenger side of his car and opened the door. I slid into the seat, and he closed the door behind me. Inside, I noticed he'd done an outstanding job of detailing the interior; everything gleamed.

He sat in the driver's seat. "Sorry, I know it's not a limo," he said.

"Limos are overrated."

"Do you like the corsage?"

"It's perfect, thank you."

He started the car. "I made dinner reservations at The Caboose. I hope that's okay."

"It sounds great. I've never eaten there but hear it's delicious." I looked out the window. Mom and Alice stood in the driveway, waving and watching us back onto the street.

"So that's Alice," he said.

"She's thinking the same about you right now."

"Do you think I passed?"

"Dressed like that? Oh yeah."

"This old thing?" He made a mocking gesture.

I laughed. "I know, right?"

He reached across the console and took my hand, suddenly serious. "Really, you look beautiful, Olivia. Your hair, your eyes—I'm just going to stare at you all night. I hope you don't mind."

I gulped. "Um, okay."

He began to rub his thumb softly across the palm of my hand, sending sparks up my forearm. I bit my lip.

Without releasing my hand, he reached forward and turned on the radio to the local country station. He then continued brushing that thumb back and forth across the palm of my hand, never letting me go. The Caboose was about a thirty minute drive from my house. It was an old train car that had been converted into a restaurant, and because of its small size, reservations were difficult to get, especially on a big event night like the prom.

"How did you get this reservation?" I asked.

"I made it a couple of weeks ago."

"But you just asked me to go to the prom with you last weekend."

It was his turn to blush. "I'd been planning it for weeks. I just didn't get up the nerve until last weekend."

"Well, that was optimistic of you—to make a reservation before you even had the date."

"Hopeful," he said, pulling into a parking spot. "I am a hopeful guy. And see? It worked out. You're here."

He opened his door and released my hand. I reached for the handle.

"Wait," he said. He exited the car, circled the back, and came around to open the door for me.

"Such a gentleman," I said.

"A romantic evening is what you wanted for your prom," he said, "and a romantic evening it shall be."

He took my hand again, and we walked up the stairs to the hostess station. After looking up our reservation, the hostess led us to our table along the window.

Everything looked so fancy. White linen tablecloths, candlelight, menus in thick black binders—this was not the diner. Nor diner prices.

"Order whatever you want," Ross said, as if reading my mind.

"Holy cow, it's so expensive here." I skimmed the offering for the cheapest dish.

"I'm having the lobster tail and petite filet."

Definitely not the cheapest dish.

Our server arrived. "May I get you something to drink?" she asked.

"Water for me," I said quickly.

"Same," Ross said.

After she left, I kept reading the menu. The idea of ordering a meal from this place and eating the whole thing filled me with dread. I thought about going for an extra-long run tomorrow to burn the calories, no matter how weak I felt. I thought about eating nothing but chicken broth and hard-boiled eggs for a couple of days.

No, I was done with all of that. I hadn't lost weight all week, which was progress. I'd gained one pound only. That one pound frightened me. It felt more like ten. It felt like I might be losing control of everything or might be giving something up that I couldn't afford to lose.

"So what are you getting?" Ross asked.

"What you suggested sounds good."

The waitress returned with our drinks. "Are we ready to order?" she asked.

"I think so," Ross said.

After answering all her questions about how we'd like our steaks cooked, what sides we wanted, and which dressing on our salads, she finally disappeared again with a promise to bring bread.

"So now that we found the cave, do you think I'll ever convince you to put on a helmet and go underground with me?" he asked.

"I don't think so. The idea just makes me feel claustrophobic."

"Tell you what. Let me take you to a big one. No crawling, no helmet, no flashlights, no spiders. Just upright walking with a real tour guide."

I knew about commercial caves from the research I'd done. "Where?"

"I want to surprise you. We'll take a road trip, just the two of us."

"A road trip, huh?"

"Yeah." He flashed that crooked, goofy smile.

"Because you're a hopeful guy?"

He lowered his deep voice. "And you are a curious girl."

I laughed. "Yes, I am."

Our first round of food arrived. I stared at the Caesar salad and bread basket. Be brave. It's only food, normal food.

I picked up the salad fork and set to work. It was delicious. The lobster tail and steak came out, and it tasted wonderful, too. My steak was cooked to perfection.

"Did you save room for dessert?" our waitress asked.

Not a chance. I shook my head. "No, thank you."

"You sure?" Ross asked.

"You go ahead. I literally have no room."

"I think we're finished," he said.

After paying the check, we headed to the dance. A photography booth was set up near the entrance to the school, and we stopped to pose for one more picture. Then we followed the music into the gym. White balloons and streamers hung everywhere. Ross led me to a table where he introduced me to a couple of his friends and their dates. While we were still standing beside them, a slow song began to play.

"Want to dance?" Ross whispered in my ear.

I nodded, feeling shy around all these new people.

Ross put his hand on my lower back and guided me toward the dance floor. Other couples gathered to sway to the ballad. His touch felt gentle and warm. When we reached the middle of the group, he took my hand and turned me toward him. I wrapped my arms around his shoulders, and we began to sway together to the music, clumsy at first. I closed my eyes, inhaled the smell of his shampoo or body wash, something faintly masculine. In the thin fabric of my dress, I felt every inch of heat from his body pressed against mine, and his breath rolled down my bare neck like a caress.

When the song ended, we stopped moving, and Ross shifted so that his hazel eyes were gazing into mine. His hands slid up my sides slowly, left my body, and then cupped my cheeks. He brought his lips closer to mine, then stopped. He brushed his thumb along my face. "Do you want me to kiss you?"

"Yes." I closed my eyes and tilted my chin upward, and after a moment, his lips pressed against mine, sending currents through my body. The kiss deepened, and his hands left my cheeks so that his arms could crush our bodies together. My hands found their way into his curls. It was as if we were alone in the woods instead of on a crowded dance floor, at least until one of his friends stopped to say, "Get a room, you two."

We separated, both of us shaken by the intensity of what had happened.

"Get out of here," Ross growled, giving his friend a shove, but laughing.

He took my hand again. The band played fast music. When had that changed? I followed him off the dance floor to the table we'd claimed. We sat, and he refused to let go of my hand the rest of the evening, and every time we danced, we snuck more kisses.

After the dance ended, we boarded busses that took us to Nashville for our after-prom party on a historic paddlewheel riverboat. Tickets cost extra, but Ross insisted that we go—his treat. It was senior prom. We'd never have another chance for a trip like this.

When we boarded the ship, they greeted us with a live band, tables of hot and cold appetizers, and candlelit tables everywhere. On the upper deck, we could sit under a velvety canopy of stars and moonlight while music played beneath our feet. That's where Ross and I spent the first hour of the cruise, just talking and enjoying the breeze and sights as the ship cruised the Cumberland River and passed the skyline of downtown Nashville.

After awhile, people started coming upstairs with plates of food. "Let's go check out the buffet," Ross said.

"Okay."

Shrimp cocktail, fried chicken tenders, beef tenderloin, chips and spinach artichoke dip, tiny quiches, and dozens of other appetizers tempted us from the table. The spread of food looked artful—and terrifying.

So many calories.

I didn't know what to do around all that food. Ross put several chicken fingers on his plate and drizzled honey mustard over them. He reached for the shrimp and then paused, realizing that I hadn't picked up a plate.

"Is everything okay?" he asked.

"I just—I don't know where to start."

He looked at the table as if seeing it for the first time. As if he could see it through my eyes, and understand. He put his arm around me.

"Close your eyes," he said.

I did. I trusted him completely.

"What's your favorite thing at the diner? If you wanted me to cook something for you, what would it be?"

I smiled. "Sorry, but my favorite thing is Mrs. Lee's strawberry pie. I'm not sure you can bake as well as she can."

"Hmm, we'll have to see about that one day. But right now, let's concentrate on strawberries. I'm going to feed you some of those. Would you like chocolate with that?"

I remembered the chocolate fountain. "Yes, please."

Keeping my eyes closed, I waited. Presumably, he selected a couple of strawberries and dipped them in the fountain.

"Okay, what's your second favorite thing at the diner?" he asked.

Eyes still closed, I said, "I do like the chicken tenders. You could fry up some of those, cook."

He chuckled. "Coming right up. Anything else?"

"I had a huge dinner. I think that's enough for now."

"Okay, you can open your eyes again." He handed a plate to me. Three chocolate-covered strawberries were arranged around some chicken tenders.

"Thank you," I said.

"You want to sit outside or inside?"

"Definitely outside."

He put his hand around my waist, where it rested warm and wonderful, and we walked up the stairs to the second story of the ship. We sat at an empty table. A candle flickered inside a glass bowl, and strings of white lights decorated the railings. Soft music played on the speakers.

I looked at my plate of food. It seemed very daunting.

"Here, let me help you," Ross said. "May I?" He reached across the table for one of the strawberries, hesitating above one. I nodded, and he picked it up. I let him place it in my mouth.

"Is this enough romance for you?" he whispered as I chewed the chocolate treat.

I swallowed and smiled at him. "Oh, yes."

May 24

Dress warm had been Ross's advice for our excursion to his secret location, and I'd chosen comfortable jeans and a long-sleeved cotton shirt. My hair was pulled up in a ponytail. Outside temperatures ran in the eighties, but he warned that the cave stayed in the fifties year round. In the summer, people often visited wearing shorts and froze. Not us.

We arrived at the park just after noon. A few cars occupied spaces in the parking lot. Rocky hills of pine and hardwood trees surrounded the picnic pavilion. Ross took my hand, and we walked the short distance to the lodge to purchase tickets for the tour.

It was a gorgeous stone and log building. Rocking chairs sat on the broad porch, and a fountain splashed on the patio. While Ross went to the cashier, I looked around.

I turned and suddenly spotted the mouth of the cave.

It was a humongous yawn of blackness under a lush green hillside. Mist floated lazily near the entrance, and people lingered under the tall archway. They looked miniscule in comparison.

Ross joined me. "Impressive, isn't it?"

"I can't believe it."

"Here's your ticket. The tour starts in five minutes." He took my hand again and kissed my palm. I looked at him.

"Thank you for bringing me here."

"Don't thank me yet," he said. "You haven't even seen the good part."

"*That's* not the good part?" The entrance of the cave was magnificent.

"It's called *Cathedral Caverns* for a reason. Just wait." He twisted his fingers around mine and squeezed.

We wandered down the steps to wait for the tour guide. Ross dropped my hand and wrapped his arms around my middle, pulling me close against him. My ribs felt too hard and prominent against his arms, even though I'd been gaining weight and getting stronger.

On our drive here today, we'd stopped at a fast food restaurant—my old favorite. I'd eaten a small order of curly fries, savoring the spiraling ringlets and gobs of ketchup. I ordered a Diet Coke, not regular, but progress was progress. Ross knew how hard I was trying.

I'd even stopped posting on the Blubber Busters boards. I missed my friends there but knew that community wasn't healthy for me if I was going to stop dieting. I didn't weigh myself anymore. It was incredibly scary. I was trying to be courageous.

A woman wearing a park uniform passed through the group. "Okay, folks, are ya'll ready to get started?" Her southern drawl was very thick.

221

We nodded eagerly.

"Follow me, then."

We entered the cave. The temperature immediately began dropping, and mist swirled around us. Darkness descended. The cool, damp air felt good after standing in the humid sunshine in jeans and a long-sleeved shirt.

We walked down a long slope and gathered as a group at the bottom of a huge room, where the park guide took our tickets.

"Cathedral Caverns has the widest entrance of any commercial cave in the world," she said, gesturing back at the huge arch we'd just passed through. "That's twenty-five feet tall and one hundred and twenty-eight feet wide."

She went on to tell us about the Native American Indians that had inhabited the cave and the remains that had been found at the mouth during archaeological excavations. The cave held four world records, which she would show us on the tour. I looked at Ross. No wonder he liked this stuff; it was interesting. He smiled and squeezed my hand.

As we followed the wide path, our guide narrated a story of the cave's history: how it was discovered, when it changed hands from various private owners, when the State of Alabama acquired it for a state park, and what formations we saw. We stopped at the largest column formation in the world, named Goliath. The lighting, reflection pools, and coloring made the entire room seem other-worldly—like we were on another planet.

Next we crossed over Mystery River and saw another world record—the largest flow stone wall. It looked like a giant waterfall made entirely of stone.

We walked slowly, giving everyone time to keep up. Our tour guide was funny and told anecdotes that kept things entertaining as well as informative. A child in our group, perhaps five years old, kept answering questions as though the tour was just for her. The adults laughed.

As Ross had suggested, the climax was the cathedral room. More stalagmites, stalactites, and columns than you could possibly count were clustered together in a colorful display of wonder. I stared, open-mouthed. The path wound through the room, back and forth, up and around. Accent lighting highlighted the most impressive formations. It was all too much to take in at once.

I couldn't believe that something like this existed beneath the earth's surface, that in this place where there ought to be mud and bedrock, we could witness such beauty.

The tour stopped at a cliff where the guide turned out all the lights to allow us to experience "total darkness." Beyond the railing, there was still almost three thousand feet of cave that wasn't accessible to the public because it was under private land.

On the return walk, the guide told us to go at our own pace. The talking part of the tour was over.

"What did you think?" Ross asked.

"It's amazing down here. I loved all the formations and the stories. No wonder you enjoy this so much!"

"So are you ready to visit a wild cave with me?"

I wondered what things might be hiding in the one we'd found on his grandfather's farm. It seemed such a shame that I'd wandered all over those hills, looking for the cave, but I was too afraid to go inside and discover what secrets it might hold.

"Maybe," I said. "I'd love to explore the cave that we found."

"I wouldn't take you in that one first," Ross said. "*I* don't even know what's down there. It's too dangerous for a beginner. I need a guide to map it first."

I gave him a disappointed pout.

"But I appreciate your enthusiasm," he added. "I'll take you into some of the best caves I've been to so far."

"Okay. And once you've mapped out ours, you'll take me there?"

"Deal."

We crossed the bridge over Mystery River again. That trickle of water was the great whittling force that had created much of the surrounding cavern. The river looked harmless now, but the guide said that during especially heavy rain storms, it had been known to flood the cave. The high-water mark was easy to see.

Finally we returned to the massive cave entrance. What had the guide said? Twenty-five feet tall and one hundred and twenty-eight feet wide. Emerging from the depths of the cave and suddenly seeing that bright opening up ahead was a startling view. Mist swirled around the damp rocks.

My elbow knocked against my hard rib cage. My hip bones still jutted out through my jeans like a pair of first place trophies in my weight loss contest. I released Ross's hand and stopped. For a moment I felt sad to leave the darkness of this place. I'd grown comfortable. Even though I could see the way out, even though it was right there in front of me, I knew how easy it could be to stay willingly lost in this hollow beauty.

Yes, it was lovely down here, but it was also small, cold, and hard as stone. The beauty that existed out there was expansive and warm, as big as the whole wide world.

Grabbing Ross's hand and holding tight, I walked beside him, up the slope, and into the sunlight again.

Discussion Questions

1. From what sources of information does Olivia draw her ideas about "True Love," and how does that help or hinder her in her own relationships?
2. Why does Olivia decide to lose weight? How does this reason change over time?
3. How would you characterize Olivia's diet? Is she an anorexic? Why or why not?
4. What influence, if any, do you think the absence of a father plays in Olivia's life?
5. Discuss the symbolism of caves in building the main themes of the novel?
6. Early in the story, Olivia identifies herself as a tomboy and athlete. In what ways do her ideas about beautify conflict with her self-identification? When she begins losing races to become thin, do you think she sees the conflict? Why or why not?

7. Going to the prom seems very important to Olivia. Why? What do you think the prom represents to her?

8. Describe the important elements of Olivia's friendships with Alice, Tammy, Ross, and the girls on the Blubber Busters boards. How does each of them influence her?

9. Losing too much weight often leads to lying and hiding under baggy clothes to avoid questions from friends and family. No one except Alice confronted Olivia forcefully. Why do you suppose others shied away from pushing the issue?

10. Olivia's friend tells her that Brody is a cheater. Yet she keeps her friendship with Ross a secret from him. Does this make her a cheater too?

11. Olivia uses the adjective "strong" to describe herself. By the end of the story, do you think she is a strong girl? Why or why not?

12. How is Olivia's experience similar to those of other girls with eating disorders? What makes her different?

13. In what ways has Olivia changed by the end of the story?

Acknowledgements

I'm deeply grateful to my editor, Beth Bruno, for her thoughtful suggestions and careful eye. Any errors are my own proofing mistakes during final production.

I also want to thank Kelsey Crafton for designing the cover artwork.

Finally, much love and appreciation to my husband for urging me to pursue independent publishing. Without his encouragement, my novels would continue to reside only on my hard drive.

Khristina Chess lives with her husband and numerous pets in Huntsville, Alabama. By day, she is a harried, Diet Mountain Dew-jazzed manager at an international software company, but in the wee hours of the morning, she writes novels. Visit her online at www.khristinachess.com.

Made in the USA
Coppell, TX
10 August 2022

81260228R00135